About the Author

Mr Prabhakaran was born in Kalliad, a remote village in Kerala, on twenty-three April 1957. He is the eldest son of a farmer who has eight children. His education came with great adversity. However, he graduated from Calicut University at the age of twenty. Later, he took an MA degree from Kerala University, accepted the profession of a teacher at Chapparapadavu high school, read Shakespeare and the classics, wrote stories and articles. As a social worker and activist, he worked among the community for equality and against caste discrimination. His wife is Rema. He has two daughters, Aparna and Nihara, pursuing studies.

Upon the Hillock

Prabhakaran V V

Upon the Hillock

Olympia Publishers
London

www.olympiapublishers.com
OLYMPIA PAPERBACK EDITION

Copyright © Prabhakaran V V 2023

The right of Prabhakaran V V to be identified as author of this work has been asserted in accordance with sections 77 and 78 of the Copyright, Designs and Patents Act 1988.

All Rights Reserved

No reproduction, copy or transmission of this publication may be made without written permission.
No paragraph of this publication may be reproduced, copied or transmitted save with the written permission of the publisher, or in accordance with the provisions of the Copyright Act 1956 (as amended).

Any person who commits any unauthorised act in relation to this publication may be liable to criminal prosecution and civil claims for damage.

A CIP catalogue record for this title is available from the British Library.

ISBN: 978-1-80439-282-9

This is a work of fiction.
Names, characters, places and incidents originate from the writer's imagination. Any resemblance to actual persons, living or dead, is purely coincidental.

First Published in 2023

Olympia Publishers
Tallis House
2 Tallis Street
London
EC4Y 0AB

Printed in Great Britain

Dedication

I hereby dedicate this novel to my late father, PVK Nair, Kalliad.

Acknowledgements

I sincerely thank all my teachers who taught me English at schools and colleges and led me to the world of literature, especially Sri PK Sukumaran Nambiar, J Francis, and K Ismail. My sincere thanks to Prof AM Kamalam Ramakrishnan, Rtd Prof and HOD of English, Payyannur College, Payyannur, for the guidance she has rendered in making the novel a perfect one. Again, my sincere thanks to Sri Sudhakaran K and Risastech, Balussery.

Chapter 1

As usual, the rivulet down the '*Kudiyatti*'[1] rushed to meet its lover, flowing over the slippery mossy rocks and luminescent in the rising sun. The songs of the cuckoo escorted. As it was springtime everywhere, the trees and shrubs blossomed, fragrant and stimulating. A gentle breeze showered flowers along with the dead leaves of *Terminalia alata*. The beetles, gay and humming, roamed from one blossom to another in search of honey and pollen grain. The bees were active and darted to blossoms frequently. The rising sun made the hills golden. The rivulet frothing and silvery jingling the bells on the Ghanjira.

Kodanddi looked into the snares that he had put up the previous day. The golden beams made the slushy green thicket colourful. He went into the thick and dark thicket, which showered dew on him, along with petals and pollen. He appeared cupid, peduncles showering the petals as though they were horripilate. Walking stealthily, he reached them. Having found nothing, he felt frustrated. His fairly black body was spotted with silvery and golden-laden coolness and fragrance.

The little cloth he wore on his waist had been rolled up and over. The thorns of *Acacia intsia* had scratched his thigh and bloodied his privates. Plucking some leaves of the *pacha chedi*[2] and scraping between his palms, he made the spicy, fragrant essence drop on the bruises. He writhed and wriggled and rolled in pain.

---

[1] A small village on the western ghat.
[2] a medicinal herb, Neurocalyx calcinus.

Sitting on a fallen log, he thought about the bad luck of the day for a while. Nothing had been snared in. He would have to return to his barn empty-handed, causing much annoyance to his aged parents.

They would be waiting gnawingly hungry, crouching on the palm mat spread in the open space to get the warmth of the rising sun into their bones or pounding the Areca nut with a pestle and mortar. The burning having subsided, he resumed through the porcupine path rather easier than the thorny thicket. A perdix rufer couple flew away, chirping as if bewildered or they didn't like intruders turning up to dampen their joy in their capricious rambling. His darts would have pierced them, but he restrained.

He didn't know whether the rufers were edible or not. The sun had risen considerably high in the meantime, and the wildlife had begun their daily routine. The reptiles crawled after their prey. The wild fowls scratching at the earth and pecking at the pests and worms in the thickets cooed and seemed frightened. Seeing the stranger, a chameleon chattered.

Kodanddi covered his navel with his left palm as it could suck blood even while it was darting. He saw its neck was bloodied, and it seemed satisfied over its unexpected luck and blinked at him.

Kodanddi couldn't help but be excited by the fragrant *Mimusops elanji*. His nostrils expanded as he appreciated its intoxicating fragrance. But soon he was taken aback. A cobra was creeping on the dry leaves. The thick foliage of *Mimusops* had become a dark, cool shelter to the reptiles; moving in and out of the termite mounds and pecking the termites appeared drastic, but beautiful to him.

The foothill valley was so steep that Kodanddi crawled on his haunches to go down the precipice. Yet he wished to go down deep as he knew the hedgehogs were abundant in the recesses. The thorns of the *Acacia intsia* spread over the thicket hooked him in several places, and blood oozed out, fretting and fuming his body.

He had made smoke to suffocate the hedgehog at the mouth of the burrow with coconut fibre the previous day and enclosed the nest. Unable to bear the suffocation, the animal might jump out of the burrow but right into the nest; struggling would make the animal more and more entangled, or sometimes the nest would be broken, and the animal could escape, making the whole process futile.

Kodanddi prayed to the deity on the mountain that such an ill luck wouldn't have happened and offered obsequies to it. He breathed heavily as he reached nearer to the mouth of the cave, the most dreadful it had become. It appeared like a little battlefield, the plants and shrubs being desecrated as if something might have rolled on it; the nest had been torn to pieces and lost. He became disheartened. Yet he wondered for a moment how big the animal would be!

Strongly dejected, he sat on a rock. Fear slowly overcame him, and a numbness affected his body. He wished he had some company. The loneliness and fear made him resume his surveillance, for he didn't want to be there alone.

At the foot of the hill was a small valley covered with plants, and creepers blossomed. The breeze laden with fragrance and pollen grain patted him. His nostrils expanded as if to assimilate the fragrance of the landscape.

Dragonflies and beetles were on the blossom, sucked honeydew, and were happy and gay. Wild music made him alert, along with the rivulet frothing, silvery white gushed down to the Kudiyatti.

Kodanddi stepped into the rivulet, and icy-cold crystal clear water made him horripilate. As he washed his body, his bruises still pained him and trickled out blood drops, but slowly he felt refreshed and comfortable. Assimilating the quintessence of the herbs growing in abundance on the slushy green hill, it might have acquired the power to cure even the old bruises.

The mossy rocks were slippery, but water trickled crystal-clear and luminescent. The gentle breeze pacified him.

Forgetting the ill luck of the day, Kodanddi watched the greenery of the hills demarked by the silvery water flows that resembled the silver linings on the green silk woven by the earth, the blue sky stretching like an umbrella over the blossom trees colouring beautifully.

Time was endless as he stood gazing at the green hills decorated by the blossom trees. Amidst the music of the water flowing and the birds chirping, he heard a feeble, groaning sound, probably let out by a human, which made him shudder.

"A human being," he exclaimed. He looked around. "Isn't it a human cry that I heard?" he said to himself, looking around.

"Oh! No, how could it be? Here in these dense woods!"

He couldn't sense the least possibility of it. But he heard the weak groaning sound again. It was feebler than before.

A lonely fear began to overpower him. Yet climbing on a big rock, he looked around and noticed a hut on stake-like things woven by palm leaves not so high as usual, but at the height of a man. It had a dangling ladder in a rosewood tree.

He hadn't noticed it the other day when he had come to put up the snare. "Who would be in the barn dying?"

A human being must have been abandoned in the woods amidst wild animals and reptiles, he concluded.

He determined to take a look. working his way through the

bushes, Kodanddi moved towards the barn. Under the stakes, the ground was fully covered by *Intsia*, whose thorns would prevent reptiles and wild boars from entering the hut.

As he came nearer, his heart beat faster, and he could hear the groaning more clearly than before.

An unbearable stench prevailed around the barn and seemed to him to be emitted by a rotten corpse left by the tigers. But the groaning noise was a clear indication of life, he thought.

Kodanddi approached the barn. Pushing the reed screen open, he peeped in and was shocked; the sight was drastic, yet he couldn't flee. Daring himself, he looked at the human figure.

"An abandoned angel or goddess of the woods," he exclaimed. No, probably a woman with furuncles all over her body. Some were dark red, but some were like ripe gooseberry; not an inch of her fair complexioned body was unaffected. It looked like '*Vasoorimala*'[3].

The sumptuous dark curly hair, queenly shape and colour made him think she was an abandoned princess. Some of the ripened furuncles had burst, oozing pus with blood stains. She could not open her eyes or move, but she breathed; the only sign of life in her. It seemed to him that she wouldn't survive. But he couldn't do anything alone. Kodanddi left the celestial female, making sure to latch the reed screen. As he hasted, he prayed to God not to be so cruel to the prettiest thing on this earth. He feared she would cease to exist without food and water. Slowly, it began to pain him to the bottom of his heart. Though blackened a little by grief more than by the sharp pain of the deadly furuncle, he could spectate the nobility.

"Something should be done," he thought while hastening to his home.

---

[3] A theyyam representing the goddess of smallpox.

He could easily conceal a little frustration over his empty-handedness by revealing everything to his parents.

"Give her rock salty millet porridge," Chavinian told his son as he was pummelling the Areca nut with quicklime smeared betel leaves in a small mortar.

Vellachi, his mother, was sitting beside him. She rose and wobbled to the kitchen. "Otherwise, she will die," Chavinian said. Then he called out to his wife, "Vellachi. Is there millet left in the pot – gourd?" he said.

"Oh, sure. There would be some, I think," she said.

"But it should be pounded," she muttered unhesitatingly as she went to the store room.

Vellachi found the Pot of Gourd and poured the contents into a wooden mortar, and began to pound it with the pestle.

As she pounded the millet, her breast rhythmically oscillated along with her thodas. Collecting the pounded millet in a sieve, she began to winnow it.

In the meantime, Kodanddi had brought some drinking water from the spring in an earthen pot.

After setting a fire in the grate using fagots and twigs, she placed the earthen vessel with water in it, cleansing the grain with water several times. She put the millet grain in the vessel using a ladle, and shook it well. Then she covered it with its lid and waited for it to boil.

When the gruel was ready, she poured it out in a cleaned spathe to make it cool, mixed it with a pinch of powdered rock salt and filled a small pot gourd.

Kodanddi was on the thorns, for he yearned to return to the barn as soon as possible. "Feed her with a leaf spoon," Vellachi said. Her face lit up when she said it, and they looked at each other.

There was no time to lose. Kodanddi took the porridge and spathe, didn't forget to pluck two or three leaves from a nearby jackfruit tree, and speedily returned to the barn. He was careful with the porridge because he had found the path slippery and the barn difficult to reach. Once or twice, the gourd shell was about to fall off, but he didn't let it. The gentle wind bearing the coolness and fragrance caressed him. He was panting and sweating and so caught up in his quest that he never heard the jingling of nature's anklet, the waterfall, or the chirping of birds. Neither the blossom trees or the copulating birds stood in his way, like a dart heading towards its aim, not minding anything on the way, he headed to where he had found her.

On entering the barn, he found her in the same position as earlier, the groaning less frequent and even more feeble, the signs of life evident but ready to cease at any time.

He fetched water from a rivulet nearby, sprinkled it on her face, and blotted it with a piece of cloth for fear that wiping would burst the furuncles.

She tried to open her eyes, but in vain. Kodanddi felt pity. He sat beside her, placing her head on his lap. With a wet cloth, he removed the rheum from her eyes. The stench became unbearable, and he felt like vomiting. The putrification of the furuncles making his lap wet was disgusting. He made her open her lips and, scooping the porridge from the swathe with a jackfruit leaf spoon, he dripped it into her mouth. She couldn't swallow it easily, but he continued to feed her.

"Gulp it," he beseeched in a low voice. Struggling, she swallowed it down. The second time it was not as difficult as before. Slowly, he dripped the porridge into her mouth until she was reluctant to take any more.

He kept the remaining gruel for the evening and closed the

lid of the gourd shell. Then he poured some water into her mouth for gargling. She had no energy to spit it out, but it went in slowly. He blotted her lips. He could feel her inner throbbing though she was totally alien to him. She tried to open her eyes, and when she finally managed to get them half opened, he could see they were beautiful and alluring, like lotus petals. But soon, teardrops appeared at the inner corner, which he blotted away slowly. He put her head down on the palm mat and got up, allowing her to rest.

It seemed to him that she wanted to say something, but the sheer fatigue restrained her from doing so. Thoughts seemed to flash through her worried mind as she tried to string the sequence of events together that had left her abandoned; however, she kept fainting, which prevented her from managing this. The sad turn of events might be haunting her.

Washing the swathe in the rivulet, he kept it for the next day, and before latching the reed door, he looked at her. She, too, with eyes half open, glanced at him. A feeble, pale smile appeared on her face.

It pained him to leave her alone. He felt guilty about it. Fearing the dreadfulness of the disease, he couldn't take her to his hut. Moreover, he was alone.

Half-heartedly, Kodanddi reached home. Four or five people were discussing the matter with his father, who had been sent word by him.

"A royal lady has been found in the woods abandoned," Chavinian told them. "Is it proper to abandon the indisposed in the woods?" he said.

They shook their heads as a mark of disagreement.

"Then bring her here. We'll treat her." Chavinian's words were true and firm like a rock.

"Who is this person?" Kothumban eagerly said.

"A royal lady, perhaps a princess," Chavinian said, inferring his son's words. "Shall we throw her away in the woods, making her easy prey to the wild beasts passing by?"

His anger was mounting.

"The woods are our homes. If any dreadful disease comes to our home, what will we do?"

Raising this question, Chavinian looked around for a quick response.

"Let's bring her here." Kothumban cast his eyes to the corner at Kodanddi and smiled.

Everyone agreed to this.

Vellachi gave them black tea in earthen bowls. Then she said, "Bring her here before dark."

"You needn't be afraid," Chavinian asserted.

"If it is treated once, it won't come again at all."

Accordingly, a litter was made using bamboo and vines. Examining its strength, Chavinian said, "You shouldn't loiter, make haste."

"Take care, the footpath is slippery, and further carrying her uphill in a litter would be hazardous," Chavinian told them.

Carrying the litter, five of them set off during the mid-day sun.

There would be rain in the evenings during this season. If it rained, the journey would become too tiresome on the slippery footpath, Kodanddi thought while hastening down through the steep woods.

The thick foliage of leaves provided a cool shade for them, and the trees dropped withered flowers and dead leaves everywhere.

An unprecedented fear haunted them, for they heard movement, like scratching on a copper cauldron.

They shuddered and stopped abruptly.

"It's the growling of a big cat," Kothumban said, trembling.

"It's a long way off," Kodanddi consoled them. "We have come very near, just a short distance from her now," he continued.

Drumming noisily on a tin-coated iron vessel, they advanced, Kodanddi in front shouting while the others followed.

"The rotten smell might incite the beasts," Kodanddi said to himself while his body throbbed in pain.

They heard her groaning at a distance, and Kodanddi inferred that nothing untoward had happened to her.

Chapter 2

The old couple began to make hectic arrangements to receive the distinguished guest as related by their son. They cleared the chayippu arranged a temporary cot made of stripped areca, covered with a mattress filled with Neem leaves. Vellachi also put some gum frankincense on live coal taken in an earthen bowl. Then she began to cook millet porridge.

In the meantime, many came from nearby huts, men with long sticks chewing betals, half cladded; some were leading their pets; and women with naked breasts, especially young women with plump breasts bobbing, and hiding behind their mothers and children wiping the mucus on their naked shoulders.

"It's highly infectious, so go away," Chavinian told them to quit because the outcast queen carried a dreadful infectious disease. They fled, murmuring disgustedly. The shouting of men carrying the litter could be heard at a distance, and Chavinian walked up and down his courtyard, making sure that nobody remained except the two of them, yet some peeped from behind the trees in the woods, eager to know who was it that was honourably being transferred.

The litter was taken directly to chayippu, and the men made her lie on the mattress. They latched the reed door and left, leaving them alone. The overpowering stench pervaded everywhere, making them sick.

Vellachi put some more gum frankincense in an earthen bowl with living coal. Soon the perfumed smoke overpowered the stench, temporarily giving them respite.

Vellachi boiled water putting black catechin in it. Daring to enter into chayippu, she made the girl drink, drop by drop, and sat beside her, caressing gently on her forehead.

The fever had subsided, but the furuncles had not completely settled.

She half opened her eyes and looked at Vellachi. Surprisingly, tears began to trickle down her cheeks, making her upper clothes wet.

She didn't say anything. A sea of emotions might have gushed in her turbulent mind. Blotting her tears, Vellachi told her, "Don't cry."

But she couldn't control the tears because of the stinging pain. Nor could she console herself, finding fault with her ill fate. The intense grief burst out, and nobody could have stopped it. Actually, they were not teardrops but drops of life blood oozing out from her heart.

As the days passed, the furuncles settled, and the pus dried up, sneak and cramp yet less unbearable than the wounds to her mind. It all appeared like a juggling act to her as scene after scene flashed through her sub-conscious mind. There she lay abandoned, motionless and fluttering in a semi-conscious world.

Vellachi brought the millet gruel propreitic in mixing the rock salt, a condiment made of Aloe leaves and raw turmeric that tasted bitter, making her vomit. Yet she felt compelled to gulp two or three lumps in order to live.

Vellachi wiped her lips and face with a wet cloth. Leaving her to rest, she walked away. Like the hairy aril moving about in the wind, the latter floated, ruminating on past events.

The red rays of the setting sun awakened her. She opened her eyes. The sun was going to set. She could see the red globe disappearing slowly, leaving the earth and its inhabitants in the dark, through the breach of the palm leaves, certainly a magnificent and fantastic revelry. The horizon in the west was painted reddish golden, the sun brightening the fragments of the clouds glittering slowly as it sank behind the mountain.

The shadows grew longer and darker, resembling the scenes of a shadow play to her.

Vellachi brought oil lamps, small earthen *chirathus*[4], filled with Hydnocarpus pentandra oil. The wick of the lamp burnt, emitting a smell that penetrated into the nostrils. One was placed on the Verandah and another in the chayippu.

Kodanddi had come earlier that day, so unfamiliar it was to his parents. Sitting on the floor, he talked to his father, who listened to him keenly.

"Haven't the paddy become ripe?" Chavinian said to his son.

"Half ripe," answered Kodanddi.

"If it is so, it is high time for a night guard," Chavinian said.

"Then the work of the watch shed should begin tomorrow itself." Kodanddi planned for the next day.

"Won't you get anyone to help," Chavinian said.

"Kothumban may come, I think." Kodanddi trusted him so much.

Vellachi didn't like it. "The meal is ready," she announced.

They sat on the floor for supper. Rice and dhal-gram dish tasted better. There were roasted roots too, but no meat at all.

"Have you given food to that girl?" Chavinian said, looking at his wife.

"I gave her millet porridge and condiment," she said with a little annoyance

Peeling the roasted root, Chavinian devoured it with condiment, a very pungent relish as if he had been devoid of food for weeks.

Kodanddi looked at how his father ate the roots and felt pride that he could collect such delicious roots for him from the woods.

---

[4] Spoon-like earthen bowls used as oil lamps.

A cool breeze swept through, carrying the fragrance of the wild flowers and roasted roots, and the wick of the lamp almost blew out. But Vellachi protected the flame using a swathe, which reflected the light and became brighter and more focused.

Having finished supper, they washed their hands and mouths and sat munching the lime-smeared betel leaves with Areca nut pieces, spat the red fluid, placing two fingers across their lips hissing in the courtyard.

Together, they went into where the patient was lying and found that her condition had improved. The furuncles had settled completely but not healed, they helped, but the rotting smell of the pus still prevailed in the chayippu.

As if in a dream, or perhaps it might be because she heard the human voices, she opened her eyes. Seeing them, she tried to get up.

"Oh! No, don't try to get up. You're too tired," said Vellachi, seemingly happy.

The sheer fatigue had prevented her from rising. Vellachi gestured for the men to go out of the chayippu. This was to change her clothes that were soaked in urine and clean her.

Her whole body was encrusted, not an inch of intervening space on her skin remained unaffected. Fortunately, her long and sparkling eyes, like that of the musk deer, were unaffected, and Vellachi inferred from them that she would probably be from a royal family.

"Your name?" Vellachi said in a beseeching voice.

"Lakshmi, Rajalakshmi," she stammered out. Her voice was so feeble. It seemed not flexible to Vellachi.

"Shall I call you Kasthuri?" Vellachi said.

She nodded her head and said feebly. "As you like" for her, it was all alike.

"From where?"

"Kotta," she said.

Astonished and further more respectful of her, Vellachi left, nodding for her to take a rest and making sure of the reed screen latch.

Kasthuri was left alone in the chayippu. Though she had been in the woods for days, she remembered nothing, but now that she knew she was in a hut, she felt secure but anxious about her future.

As time passed, her anxiety grew, and sleep eluded her, leaving her awake all through the night.

A feeling of being lost began to haunt her as her consciousness recovered completely. It would be her fate, she thought, abandoned in the woods amidst the beasts and reptiles.

For these people, she was a closed chapter, and no one would be bothered whether she existed or not, and how long she would be afforded in the little hut was a matter of compassion, neither her right nor their obligation. But the magnanimity and generosity they gave her knew no bounds. And furthermore, those dark little figures, half-naked forest dwellers, had so much love in them ready to burst and flow out as the cool life-giving ambrosia in the rivulet flowing down unblemished and benevolent.

Vellachi didn't ask anything more, for she might have heard of the Kotta and its prowess head having the power to slaughter and destroy or to abduct any beautiful young woman whom the Mannanar had an avaricious eye on.

Nobody dared to question the uncrowned King skilled in martial arts. Vellachi had told her not to spend any more sleepless nights, for it would hamper her eyes. She had boiled coriander seeds in water to blot them up whenever she felt itching in them.

"How caring she is!" Kasthuri thought. For all these days, she fed her lovingly, treated her with ground panacea like a physician and looked after her like a maid.

Caressing slowly over her encrusted body, she thought how disgusting and horrible it would be to see herself, but there was no mirror in the hut. She couldn't see her own face for days; otherwise, she would have been shocked at the frightful sight. Perhaps it was for the better.

The itching made the crusts break; two or three fell down on the floor, fairly black which was smeared with cow dung and charcoal powder.

She could perceive now that her body was full of crusts; abundant as a black buck, white spotted deer or a leopard with dark spots.

Everybody was asleep while Kasthuri was wide awake, even in the middle of the night. A cool breeze swept in. She thought it might rain. The thunderbolt which struck and dumped her in the woods and denied everything except the air to breathe seemed too terrific to be believed. Blaming the cruel fate which didn't take her life, lamenting that even death had abandoned her. No one wanted her, not even death.

Meditating upon "*Yama*,"[5] she lay still, waiting for His footsteps to take her away from the human world.

Soon it began to bud hatred towards Kodanddi in her heart of hearts for the love and affection he had bestowed upon her.

She heard sounds coming from the kitchen. She assumed that Vellachi had awakened early to prepare food for Kodanddi and others working on the hill tract.

Having placed the firewood in the fireplace, Vellachi ignited it, placed water in an earthen pot, cleaned the rice thoroughly,

---

[5] The God of death.

washed it several times, and put it in the earthen pot on the fireplace and stirred well with a coconut shell ladle.

The eastern horizon blushed, and all the living beings on earth broke out of their homes. The woods became active. The crickets began to hum, and the birds flapped their wings and chirped. A herd of wild hogs returned to their habitats from the farmyards after sumptuously feasting on colocasia, yam and plantain. The night reptiles returned to their dens and the day reptiles went after their prey. Vellachi took some rice gruel in the ladle and squeezed it to test whether it was properly cooked to her satisfaction. Then she poured the water from the boiled rice into a '*Kanhikalam*'[6]. She waited for some time to cool it down. Then she brought the big gourd shell, washed it thoroughly, filled it with rice gruel, and put some common salt and three or four *Kandari*[7] in it. Before tightening the lid of the pot of Gourd, she didn't forget to pour some salted gooseberry water into it to make it tastier.

Kodanddi had awakened and went to the toilet behind a bush.

"Oleennu koncham bellam kondari." *("Bring some water from the rivulet"*), Vellachi asked her son when he came back.

"I'll bring it soon," Kodanddi said and left for the rivulet taking two large earthen pots, and cautiously filled them with water and brought them back to her satisfaction.

Placing the pots in the light, she examined the water to see whether there was any water leech in it. Having found nothing, she put the water pot over the fireplace, ignited the firewood, put some leaves of the Neem-tree and other medicinal leaves in it for

---

[6] The vessel used to decant boiled rice.
[7] A small chilly having a pungent taste.

the vethu, inserted some more firewood in the fireplace and blew air. Kothumban, carrying a hoe and hatchet, entered, calling Kodanddi yetta.

Kodanddi was tying the "*thodangu*[8]" on his waist.

"Sit down, Kothumban and have some kanji," Vellachi invited him for the rice gruel. She served them gruel and condiment, which they swallowed.

Hanging the chopper in the "*thodangu*" and placing the large spade and iron bar on his shoulder, Kodanddi walked ahead, carrying the gourd shell in his left hand. Kothumban followed him with his farm tools. Chavinian was still in his bed, covered with a blanket; he had been sleeping late in the mornings recently due to old age. The golden beams of the rising sun magnificently made the hillock luminescent, and the dew drops on the leaves glittered. The two figures advanced towards the hill tract. Their shadows were longer, but their prospects brighter. Neither of them talked on the way but steadily made their way through the "*Kdari*[9]" grass; bending down on the way, they reached the hill tract.

The paddy had grown up to their waist, dark green and healthy, and began to blossom along with their dreams, which also had blossomed. A gentle breeze caused a wave in the green carpet as it got identified. Kodanddi feared that the flowers might fall. The millet grew more healthily along the border. The dhal-gram flowers appeared as nose studs to women, and flowers of cucumber and golden anklet peeped through the paddy.

Looking for a suitable place to erect a watch shed, they reached where they could see the whole of their crops. Weeds were few as the paddy grew in abundance.

---

[8] The hook to be fastened to the waist to hang down the chopper.
[9] A kind of long grass.

Together they went to the woods nearby, cut wooden pillars, beams and rafters, dug holes deep enough to erect the pillars to their satisfaction, fastened beams and rafters, brought palm leaves to thatch the roof and made upper berths.

Working like well-oiled machines for hours, exhausted and hungry, they sat, drank gruel from the gourd-shell and took rest. A breeze pacified them with coolness and fragrance from the rice blossoms.

"We'll gain this year," Kothumban began to say.

"The time has gone astray. We can't expect everything to be good," Kodanddi reacted.

A reddish deer with her calf held her head high and looked at them with long, sparkling eyes; then they quickly took to their heels.

"Wild boars at night and wild goats in the daytime. How can we get along?" Kodanddi expressed his disgust.

"And birds will flock in large numbers when the paddy is at red-ripe," Kothumban said.

"Let's resume our work," Kodanddi exhorted.

They fetched Palmyra leaves to thatch the roof of the watch house. Palmyra leaves were thick and big so that they could thatch the shed comfortably.

The setting sun had painted the overcast western sky. The dark clouds, whose edges were glittering golden looked like a large black blanket embroidered with gold and silver. The flower stars of the earth smiled at it, wished earnestly to cover their nudity. Slowly, the light faded. Kodanddi and Kothumban made haste before the hillock wore the dark cloak. Two old praying hearts were anxiously waiting for them. The young girl who longed to see her saviour lay inside.

He should return home before the lighting of the dusk-lamp. Wherever he went, he was always home by this time.

They walked steadily, striking a long stick on the ground in front of them to keep the reptiles away. Taking along Kothumban with him, Kodanddi reached home late, causing much worry to his parents, but they suppressed it, resorting to sobbing, for they knew he had been working hard the whole day.

The icy cool water in the rivulet refreshed them and helped to shed off the sweat and fret of the day, filling them with fresh energy and vigour. They ate a delicious supper, especially flavoursome, a roasted salty dried pigmeat crushed on the grind stone with green Kandari chilly and coconut oil poured over; moreover, mother's love was mixed in abundance.

Chewing pan after supper was followed simply as a custom. They spat the red fluid in the courtyard. Wiping the fluid trickling down his chin, Kodanddi said:

"Mom. How is her illness?"

"Who?" Vellachi looked at him slyly.

"Kasthuri," he said.

"I made her bathe in the vethu." Then she continued, "The crusts are falling off. It is the time for spreading disease."

Chavinian interrupted at this time and said, "Raw turmeric and Neem leaves are to be made into a paste and smeared all over before taking a bath."

Kodanddi was sitting on the verandah dozing. He was sinking in a sea of oblivion, for he had worked so hard. The bath in the serene, fresh cool rivulet and the sumptuous food might have intensified it. Kodanddi fell on the mat exclusively spread for him. Kothumban lay beside him.

Under the dim light in the lounge, her thodas glittered, and her wrinkled face shone. Vellachi saw them fall fast asleep as soon as they lay down. She closed the reed screen and lay down beside her beloved, losing herself in the sea of oblivion.

But Kasthuri lying encrusted and itching all over, felt uneasy. Devoid of sleep, the pacification of mother Nature, she turned from side to side frequently, but sleep was forbidden. Sometimes she closed her eyes tightly, but to no avail. The night seemed never ending to her. Each minute was like an age. And at midnight, how or when she didn't know, she slipped back to the extremely noisy play field of '*Muthappan*'[10]. A fast rhythm accompanied by the beating of drums and oil lamps with long handles and blue lights, babbling, giving blessings along with flowers plucked from the crown as prasadam. The paintings and designs on the face and frontlet glittered in the lamplight. His movements were vigorous but rhythmical, and he often tasted toddy and gave the devotees the prasadam. He latched the bow, aimed the arrow at the ground, and wrote something on the ground with the arrow's point.

Then the movements became swifter, and the drums reached a peak. Putting ashes, thulasi and turmeric powder on the top of her head and placing his hand there, he said, "*Konam Varanam, Konam Varanam,*"[11] to her.

"Kattilum Mettilum Anthikkum Moovanthikkum Ente ponnu Muthappa yennu vilichal aa vili Kelkkum ee Muthappan, *Andivararivario.*"[12]

Suddenly she opened her eyes. Everything had vanished, and she was left alone. Where had Muthappan gone? Where had all these pipe blowers and drum beaters disappeared? Suddenly it came to her mind that it was, after all, a dream. But she thought the dreams in the early hours of the day would come true.

The breeze in the dawn swept in. The bunches of the wild

---

[10] A theyyam common in Malabar.
[11] A kind of blessing by the theyyam. "*Goodness should come, Goodness should come.*"
[12] The ritual song sung by theyyam during the ritual dance. (In the woods and on the hills Be at dusk or at night Call me the most favourite Muthappan will hear your call God rules the world Always and everywhere.)

blossoms let the chilliness and fragrance in. Her mischievous eyes closed, and she lost herself in the cool and pleasant atmosphere. The chattering of birds could no longer be heard.

Hearing the noises of people, Kasthuri opened her eyes and thought that her dream had come true. But there was no beating of drums, nor baffling, nor the lights of the oil lamps, nor the smell of sacred turmeric.

From the human voices, she could infer that Chavinian was ailing. For days, he had been lying in bed. People from far and near had turned up to look at the dying man who had been suffering from the accumulation of phlegm.

People praised his feats as a hunter and the valour abundant in him. He had come to their rescue many times, and the abundance of love in him for his tribal people never went dry. He had taught them farming, which had been alien to them, enabled them to stand on their own feet, and be self-reliant; creating examples of his own, paved the way for prosperity. Ways of feeding cattle ventured by him had been a vast success.

The peasants had more than ten thousand tongues to compliment him. They anxiously waited for his demise, lamenting who lay on earth obstructing his breath by the phlegm.

Vellachi and Kodanddi nursed him all day and night, giving herbal medicines and wetting his lips frequently, and sat beside him with confusion in their eyes.

Soon his breathing became shallower, and then it abruptly stopped. The sun of Kudiyatti set, and darkness pervaded the hillock. There was a loud sobbing, and the people who stood nearby rushed in. A new white cloth was brought in to cover the body.

Oil lamps were soon installed. A coconut was cut into two halves. After pouring its water outside, oil was poured into the two halves, and wicks were added, ignited, and the two halves were placed, one at his head and the other at his feet.

Vellachi couldn't bear the sad demise of her lifelong companion, she had been married so long, and she sobbed so dearly enough as to make the bystanders weep slowly, which turned into a sobbing crowd.

Messengers had gone far and near, wherever there were near and dear ones, and the family were waiting for their return but could not be too long for fear that the corpse may begin to decay. Meanwhile, the preparation for the cremation had been completed to avoid further undue delay.

Waiting anxiously for the messengers to return, the day crept slowly out. Kodanddi was worried over the matter for fear that the waiting may lead to wide controversy. If they came late, the body would be ruined, which may incite feelings that an unprecedented incident would occur. If they didn't wait, the messenger and the relatives would start a riot. He would have to answer the queries.

It was a great pain to allow the corpse to ruin, and it was the same to deny the near ones to pay their last tribute. People were waiting without food and water seemingly became restless and disgusted.

Time crawled out so slowly that everyone felt each minute to be an age. The western sky slowly became red-blazed. Their shadows became longer and longer. They murmured though the pall of gloom curtailed it, but the agony grew as the mountain covered itself with a dark blanket.

When the night advanced, men and women came bearing country torches and cries of agony. Two or three still remained to turn up but had informed that they would come early in the morning as they were forbidden by mothers with newborn babies or wanted their presence at home to keep the wild beasts away.

Preparations for the cremation were being made before the

sun rose in the sky. Men started to make the funeral pyre. A pit six feet by one and a half feet was dug and was three feet deep with four openings, one at the south for the head, another at the north for the feet and the others at the central part of the pit on either side.

Two planks of coral tree of the same length as the pit were placed lengthwise on the edges of the pit filled with coconut shells. On the coral planks, seven or eight wooden logs were placed crosswise for laying the corpse. A heap of wooden logs, dried or not dried, especially that of a mango tree, was kept nearby. A bottle of ghee, a bundle of fragrant roots of cuscus grass, a dozen or more dried coconuts, camphor and agarbathies were placed at a hand's length. A country structure made of wood and vine for carrying the corpse covered in red cloth was also made.

The funeral procession began much later than the time prescribed. A team of pallbearers carried the body covered in red. Touching it, Kodanddi carried a burning country torch made of dried coconut leaves, another with some live coals in a sieve, water in a metal pot with a spout and a knife tucked in the hip.

Having circumambulated the pyre thrice, they placed the body with its head towards the south and feet to the north. Then, removing the cloth from the face, Kodanddi put grains of gold into the mouth. Others placed logs of wood on the pyre, covering it completely and supporting it with two logs on either side to keep it steady. Carrying the burning country torch, Kodanddi, followed by his kinsmen, circumambulated the pyre thrice and ignited it at the four openings. Others put camphor and other fragrant substances, poured ghee and winnowed. Soon the funeral pyre engulfed the dead body. A piece of cloth covering the body was torn and tied tightly to the knife at his hip. Soon the smell of human flesh charring spread all over the hillock. The wind took it over and carried the meaninglessness of life to faraway villages. When the pyre was burned almost completely, Kodanddi, followed by his kinsmen, sprinkled water thrice on it to make it holy, then made the sacrifice.

As part of the obsequies, "*Sanjayanam*[13]" was decided on the fourth day of the funeral. Kodanddi was to offer the "*bali*"[14] for twelve days in penance.

The women had cleansed the home, putting it in order and, having taken a bath, prepared the gruel for the men returning from the burial ground.

Having taken a bath in the rivulet, they felt relieved and refreshed and sat for the '*Kanji*'[15]. But Kodanddi could not gulp in even a spoonful.

The world had ended for him after his father's demise. He felt overwhelmed, his feelings almost bursting out as he sat with gruel in front of him for a long time.

Vellachi, too, was reluctant to consume any food and was under the service of the kinswomen. She sobbed bitterly as if someone had been plucking her heart out. The women gathered around her, too, were weeping with her, for she had been so kind and generous towards them, especially during the famine and at times of infectious disease attacks. So kind and helpful, she had robbed their hearts and filled them with love.

"Leave her alone to grieve," said someone to the thronged women. "Let her feelings be set aside by herself," he added.

She had been married a long time, and their lives had become one. No one except god could separate them; now that it

---

[13] The levelling of the pit of cremation.
[14] The ritualistic offering of boiled rice to the soul of the deceased.
[15] Rice gruel.

had happened, she was left alone in the world. She found the cascade of experiences with Chavinian from her memories bright and glittering.

Ever since she had come to live with him in his little hut, their love had never faded but was inspiring and a shining light.

But as she remembered Kasthuri, who was caged in the chayippu like a civet cat in a cage, unable to lie down or sit, and couldn't go out for the dried pus all over her body, and looked ugly and smelt foul, distressed with thirst and hunger with nobody to care for her, she heard the call of her conscience. She went to the chayippu, covered the girl's body with a long cloth dress and helped her to go to the toilet behind a bush.

A Pall of gloom prevailed over there. Since the people had been dispersed after the funeral, the home seemed haunted and lonely. Kodanddi turned the pages back. He could glimpse the anecdotes of his life. Nowhere did he find his father unloving or uncaring; instead, he was loving, responsible and innovative and never succumbed to malice.

Tears trickled down his cheeks as the memories flashed in his mind vacillating got soaked with compassion.

The bali was to begin the next morning, and Kodanddi sent word to the *parikarmi*.[16]

Early morning the parikarmi came. He brought *Karuka*[17] and flowers and leaves of *cherula*.[18] A small soil altar at the south of the courtyard was raised, sanctifying it by smearing cow dung, a tender coconut was fixed at the altar upon which the male sacrificer was to place his left knee and offer rice balls on the altar.

---

[16] the assistant in ritualistic activities in their community.
[17] a kind of grass used in the rituals.
[18] a small plant used in Bali.

Kodanddi was asked to take a bath in the rivulet soon after daybreak and was to prepare the rice for the bali. Sinking thrice in the icy cold rivulet without changing his wet clothes, he came shivering and began making the rice. In a shallow vessel made of bell metal, raw rice was taken and washed thoroughly. It was boiled and stirred well at times using a flat ladle. Once it was ready, he served it on two plantain leaves, one for the male pointing towards the south and the other for the female sacrificers pointing towards the east. In another plantain leaf was placed some pieces of karuka grass, and a karuka ring; a karuka strip tied a lewt at one end, gingalii and flowers of cherula were placed for both.

Nephews and nieces were in large numbers, though the deceased had only one son. The gorer crows had come howling, seeing the smoke in abundance. Men and women queued up to perform the bali. The parikarmi assisted.

A raw turmeric piece was rubbed on a flat stone. The turmeric paste was sprinkled on the earth mound thrice, water was sprinkled thrice to make it holy, the "karuka" grass piece was placed on the altar, it was taken back and broken into two, and again its pieces were placed on the altar, the karuka grass piece with a hook at one end was placed on the altar, again the water was sprinkled thrice, gingally was offered thrice, water sprinkled thrice, cherula leaves offered thrice, water sprinkled thrice, again turmeric paste was sprinkled on the altar. Then kneaded rice with curd was offered in three balls on the altar. Kodanddi sprinkled thrice, prostrated himself and handed over the water spout and the karuka ring to his kinsmen.

Simultaneously the ladies performed the bali on a plantain leaf turning towards the East. After the completion of the bali, all of them circumambulated the altar thrice, sprinkling water on it.

The ladies withdrew. Gents clapped their wetted hands thrice, standing in a line in front of the altar to invite the gorer crow. Again they took a bath in the rivulet and sat for the '*balikanji*'[19]. This was repeated for twelve days, and in the late hours of the twelfth night, there began the arrangements for the '*Pindam ozhukkal*'.[20]

Kodanddi took a bath in the rivulet in the middle of the night. Kothumban followed him everywhere; coming back home, they made the human form with rice and paddy and covered it with an '*anathorthu*'.[21]

Ritual lamps were placed. Kodanddi cooked the rice. Using cooked rice taken in a plantain leaf, he made the human form and performed the bali on it. Then it was placed on a bronze plate. The horoscope of the deceased and the "*bali mundu*[22]" were put in it. Then it was covered with a plantain leaf. Large oily wicks were placed on the plantain leaf after being ignited.

Kodanddi placed the bronze plate on his head and, without turning back, walked backwards until he came out of the home. Then he walked towards the rivulet, followed by others. Chanting "Govinda, Govinda… Hari Govinda."

Plunging into the water, Kodanddi set the bronze plate afloat backward, dipped himself thrice and got out; wiping the water off his body, they came back. It was all over.

For the last thirteen days, Kodanddi couldn't think of anything other than the ritual rites that would be done for the salvation of his father's soul.

---

[19] the rice gruel consumed after the bali.
[20] setting afloat the rice figure of the dead person.
[21] The new double bathing towel.
[22] A piece of cloth torn from the funeral pyre.

Chapter 3

Much earlier than the rising sun blessed the hillock with its golden beams, the gentle cool breeze woke up Kodanddi. The continued death rites and rest at home for a fortnight had made him healthier and refreshed.

The urgency of the need had made Vellachi active though she was in her mourning period. Yet she woke up early, stewed roots, ground condiment and boiled ginger coffee for breakfast.

Kothumban had told Kodanddi that he had guarded the paddy well, and it was safe from the wild boars and goats and would be better to reap at the earliest.

But a threshing floor was to be made before the reaping would begin.

As soon as Kothumban arrived with the floor levellers, one big, another small, they rushed to the hill tract. Kodanddi was eager to get there because, for nearly one month, he couldn't touch his chum plants.

On getting there, emerging from the vapidity caused by his father's demise, the murmuring of the numerous spikes played a background musical note; Kodanddi was excited.

They found a suitable spot for the threshing floor at nearly the central part of the paddy field.

"Here will do," Kodanddi said to Kothumban.

"It's almost in the middle," Kothumban said.

Together they reaped the harvest where the threshing floor was to be made and kept the sheaves of the corn nearby. Then they cleared the ground, scooped the earth with a spade and levelled. Ridges on four sides too were made.

"Shall I sprinkle water?" Kothumban asked, looking at Kodanddi.

"The earth has enough dampness," Kodanddi said, taking the big floor leveller. He began to strike the floor. Its sound stimulated the hillock and might have frightened the wild beasts, perhaps sent them to their hideouts.

"You make the ridges level," Kodanddi said to Kothumban.

He took the small floor leveller [23] and began to strike on the ridge.

Once Kodanddi completed the first round, he sat for some time, drank water and took rest.

"Sprinkle water, Kothumban," Kodanddi said.

Kothumban took two earthen pots and walked to the nearby spring. Collecting water from the spring in the big earthen pots he returned to the threshing floor, sprinkled water in such a way that the alluvial soil made a smooth surface while striking it with the floor leveller.

The second round of striking made the earth's surface smooth and glazing.

Then they waited for some time to allow the earth to go dry. The third round of strikes began after smearing cow dung. When it was completed, the floor became as smooth as the bark of the plantain and was to their satisfaction.

Looking at the western sky, Kodanddi said, "It'd be better if there is no rain at night."

Then he looked at Kothumban, who readily agreed to him.

"Oh! It won't rain today. The sky is so clear." Tying the sheaves of spikes they had reaped into two bundles, Kothumban said, "Let's go now. I'll have to return for night guard."

---

[23] The wooden implement to level and press the floor.

They cleaned the floor levellors and kept them safely away from the white ants. Putting the bundles of spikes on their heads, they headed towards their homes. "Shall we begin the harvesting tomorrow?" Kothumban said.

He would be relieved of his troublesome night guard when it was completed, he thought,

"Oh! Sure," Kodanddi readily agreed with him as a sign of appreciation for his valuable service. "The sooner we harvest, the less we will lose," he commented.

Then he said, "Didn't you call the women?"

"Of course I did," Kothumban said.

"How many would turn up?"

"It'd be at their pleasure," Kothumban said dispassionately.

"Let's make the '*Kanjee*[24]' and '*Puzhukku*'[25] here itself," Kodanddi said.

"Of course," Kothumban agreed. Then he said, "Can't it be finished in two days?" Kothumban stopped abruptly. He was so enthusiastic.

"If the reapers fall in good numbers," Kodanddi looked at him while he said it. Examining the spike that he plucked from the sheaf, he said, "This year the *chaff* is less." They felt the sheaves being weighty marked Kothumban's statement true.

Vellachi received them with a ceremonial lamp and placed the sheaf of spikes in the inner room in front of the lamp.

She didn't forget to give Kothumban the delicious root stew with condiment before he left. He ate well.

Scores of women turned up with their sickles and marched gracefully towards the hill tract. The old with wrinkled faces and grey hairs but enthusiastic; the young blushing, strutting their

---

[24] Rice gruel.
[25] Stew made out of peas or tubers.

breasts, sickles under their cloaks sparkling, but their cheeks brighter in the rising sun. Yet their collyrium eyes were bashful.

Forming up in a line, they reaped. No weeds, of course. The golden spikes bent with weight, so thick and heavy.

The women reaped the spikes and tied them into sheaves. Kodanddi and Kothumban carried them to the threshing floor from time to time, threshing the sheaves upon a flat stone to collect the paddy. The work went on stealthily and smoothly; the paddy formed into a big golden heap and became bigger as time advanced.

"Why can't you sing?" Kothumban said to the women, looking at them longingly.

They looked back at him laden with love and shyness. Their abundant breasts bashfully bobbed under their cloaks. The pigeon peas swayed their peduncles in the breeze along with that of the women. The ripened millet fanned them with their whisks.

Kodanddi and Kothumban worked so hard that no one would go by without applause.

Carrying the sheaves to the threshing ground, striking them and heaping the paddy, following by winnowing after were all carried out simultaneously.

Reaping was a festival of rejoicing. Further, the rich harvest made them enthusiastic; certainly, their hearts came out, and music flowed out along the hill tract.

Kodanddi sang. The folk women followed. The chorus echoed across the hill.

The harvesting went on effortlessly. The rendering of the song swept away their fatigue and filled them with vigour.

The women completed rows and then advanced competitively, the sheaves of spikes fluttered on the threshing ground, and the heap of paddy became bigger and bigger, which made them exuberant.

Needless to say, nobody talked about thirst and hunger until the midday sun reminded to them. Hunger and fatigue had withdrawn, paving the way for enthusiastic perseverance. Sitting on the ridges of the threshing floor, they gulped what they had brought in their bottle guards.

They were to carry the paddy home on the day itself for fear of the wild beasts. The winnowed paddy was transferred into the scores of sacks, and their openings tied. Each one of them was to carry a sack home so that transportation would be easier. Everyone agreed to carry the load.

As it was a steep mountain, it seemed to be a difficult task. Yet it was a vigorous adventure for some of the women carrying the loads on their heads, being keen and careful.

Even a slight slip might cause great harm, not only to the paddy, but to the human as well.

"Take care," Kodanddi said to the women when they walked "*Irunnu Nirangi.*"[26] Crawling on their haunches with sacks of paddy on their heads was a peerless sight.

"Have you ever heard of '*Noorumeni*'[27]?" Kodanddi had once said to Kothumban. But he couldn't convince him of the idea at that time.

But surely did he assimilate it.

"This is *Noorumeni,* Kothumban," he told him as they walked home.

To the jubilant reapers' satisfaction, the *patham*[28] was measured, and they returned home chattering happily, only to return for the next day.

Kodanddi and Kothumban were extremely excited over the

---

[26] Crawling on the haunch.
[27] Multiplying in hundred times.
[28] The cooli for reaping the harvest.

rich harvesting. "The real Mahalakshmi has stepped in," Kothumban said.

"Take as much as you need," said Kodanddi.

But Kothumban was reluctant to take any. Kodanddi gave him enough paddy to feed his family, consisting of him and his mother, for the whole year.

Kothumban looked at him with contented eyes.

Vellachi was totally discontented when Kothumban had gone to call the women to carry the paddy to his home.

She said to her son, "Sitting on your shoulder, he's eating your ear." For which she had to face a fierce look.

"No, Mother, Kothumban guarded our harvest well," Kodanddi had all the praise for him. But she retreated.

Many days had passed by without the compassionate glance of Kodanddi for which Kasthuri was waiting as a hornbill to rain. She felt abandoned or confined in a little hut like a civet cat in its cage, with nobody other than Vellachi to interact with.

Through the breach of the reed door, she had been looking for his glance, waiting for him with one thousand eyes, but never did the new moon turn up.

The red evening blaze of the sky made her cheeks red, and she felt ashamed of her fascination.

The growing darkness slowly washed out the blushes on her face. She thought that the indifference on his part might have been caused by the fear of the dreadful disease, which would take time to heal, or may be a complex that he belonged to the low-bred might have restrained him from coming, but she decided to wait for the rescuer. She knew that she had nowhere to go, going back to the Mannanar Kotta was suicidal, for the powerful and lusty man would squeeze her to sugarcane sediment.

Vellachi had more than ten thousand tongues to talk about

her son's features. During one midday doze off, Vellachi, while running her fingers through Kasthuri's hair, said, "Kodanddi is as pure as solid gold. He has no malice." Vellachi imagined her son and Kasthuri together, Kasthuri nodded as if she was listening to her. "He's valorous too." As she said it Vellachi strutted forward with pride. But her hung-down breast refused to raise, so to speak; it had no herbal medicine to rejuvenate.

Then she began to babble about his feats as a hunter. Being an expert in putting up snares; meat, fresh or dried salty, was never absent in her hut.

Kasthuri responded intermittently, which thrilled Vellachi in listing out more and more of his feats.

"My son is the prince of this mountain," Vellachi said to her one day. "No one on this hillock excels him in strength and wealth," she explained.

Kasthuri stared at her fixing her eyes on Vellachi's face; she smiled. She was pleased.

"His father had lived like a king. He had never bowed his head to anyone but had always held his head high." Vellachi began to boast, and the princess pretended to listen to her as though she had no other choice.

In the meantime, a folk of women sauntered in chattering and chewing pan, spitting the red fluid all the way and making their lips red to see the sick princess bearing the dreadful epidemic. They had been keeping away from them though it had been a rockbuster in the community circle.

The infectious period had passed, and they clamoured, eager to have a glance at her who stole the heart of the prince in their hearts.

"Where's the princess, Vellachiamma?" the folk women asked as soon as they entered the house.

"Over there, in the *chayippu*," Vellachi said, pointing towards the *chayippu*. The folk women moved towards its door.

Dazzled by the princess's look, they were amazed. She was wearing a loin cloth and an upper garment covering her plentiful breast. The abundant dark hair went down to her buttocks.

Sitting on a wooden plank, it seemed that she was thinking of her future.

Hearing the chirping of the folk women, she turned her face and smiled. The marks of the furuncles on her face hadn't diminished the beauty of her smile.

Those long and sparkling eyes half opened seemed dreaming; the parrot's beak-like nose was eager to kiss her red lips, which were slender, but the cheeks not so plump had lost lustre.

"Come in," she said.

A moment later, the folk women who were restlessly keeping outside rushed in, gathered around and began to observe her features, some touching her softly as if she were an exhibit.

Kasthuri hugged the kids and youngsters and asked them why they were reluctant to meet her.

She ran her fingers through their hair, though dishevelled and entangled, and smelling foul. While she embraced them, their breasts met. They could feel their heartbeats on each other.

For days following, there were so many visitors to her, but they cared to come neat and smart. Never did they come with entangled hair nor children with flowing mucus or smelling foul. Before they came, they had taken a bath in the rivulet, cleansed their bodies with crushed bark of *Acasia Intsia* and wore the best clothes they had.

Kasthuri never expressed ill will and treated them alike, for she believed the real beauty prevailed in the hearts, not outwardly.

The children dared to touch her, felt the smoothness of her

skin and bodily heat. Someone dared to pull her hair and the too mischievous ones lifted her upper garment and were astonished to see the two projections. Kasthuri simply sat motionless and kept on gibing at them. But slowly she became speechless.

Vellachi, though grief stricken by the death of her husband was silent but bound to her duties. She never transgressed the rules of her diet nor ignored Kasthuri's bath in the '*Vethu*'.

The marks of crusts by the feruncle were diminishing and her skin colour was returning to the original.

Vellachi believed that the prosperity had stepped into her little hut along with Kasthuri.

The abundance of the harvest meant they could survive for three or four years and this thrilled her so and she didn't want to let Kasthuri go.

Vellachi began to brew dreams in which Kodanddi was the prince and Kasthuri the princess.

The hillocks were the scenes of their ramblings. Nowadays Vellachi could easily ruminate on her revellings in the icy cold waterfalls at the lofty hillocks and in the swinging cots.

One afternoon, when everyone was dozing after a sumptuous lunch that consisted of parboiled rice kanji, steamed roots and roasted pig meat with *kandari chatney*, Vellachi opened her heart to Kasthuri.

She was looking for lice, running her fingers roughly through her Palmyra bunch hair. She said, "I want my princess girl. I won't let you go anywhere else."

Kasthuri looked at her face, embracing her she said, "How good you are!"

While embracing she could feel the motherly warmth which had been denied to her. At this juncture Kodanddi came into the *chayippu*, a rare visit, though under the same roof.

And further he would visit her in the *chayippu* only in the presence of his mother.

Kasthuri got up when she saw her saviour entering. He was astonished to see the beautiful figure standing there in front of him, undoubtedly a princess, he thought.

Their eyes collided and more than a thousand feelings flashed between them. She smiled. He too. But he seemed worried, and he spoke out, "If your illness is cured, I'll take you to your home."

A black cloud descended on her face. The smile disappeared as the dew drops on the lotus petals in her lover's anger.

"We won't let her go. Let her be here as our daughter." Vellachi's words were unusually rude, taking up the forms of a command. She feared Kodanddi would smash away her dreams.

"How can it be right?" Kodanddi said.

"Right or wrong, whatever it may be, I'm not letting her go." Her words were definite and firm.

Kodanddi was in a fix. After a while he said, "She is a princess, Mom. How she got here in the woods is a mystery."

"So what?" Vellachi raised her eye-brows.

"She doesn't belong to us." His voice wavered a little while he said it. Yet he was adamant.

But Vellachi was not ready to withdraw her claim. Justifying it unequivocally she said, "She is an outcast thrown away in the woods as food for tigers and boars. How then could the Kotta people claim her?" She was speaking at the top of her voice.

"But they would be expecting her return after her cure," Kodanddi said dispassionately, not looking at either of them.

"You got her from the forest. They had left her abandoned, leaving her to die. They'd think that she might have died, never searching for her," simple hearted Vellachi said innocently.

But Kodanddi knew that the consequences would be so terrible if something happened to her. But he said, "That is true, Mom, but do we have the right?"

"No, But…" Vellachi couldn't complete for righteousness sake.

Kasthuri sat supporting her head with her left palm. A kind of blandness soon spread on her fair sweet face. The grief trickled down her robust cheeks from her rose petal eyes. Kodanddi withdrew as he didn't want to face her and Vellachi. Retreating to the front verandah, pensive and contemplative, he said to himself, "The consequences would be great if the Mannanar knew about it."

He reclined on a sack of paddy placed on the verandah.

"He would think I was desiring Kasthuri," Kodanddi said to his mother.

"Is it wrong to give shelter to an abandoned girl?" Vellachi said.

"There is no harm in it," Kodanddi answered. But he said, "We don't have the right to keep the lost and found."

"Even if it is so, who else knows it?" Vellachi said.

"Everyone here knows it," Kodanddi said. It seemed that nobody would cause to decline his conviction.

"Is she reluctant to go back?" Kodanddi asked.

"Who else puts his head in a crocodile's mouth?" Vellachi was not ready to give up her claim.

"Yet we have to look into it." He was dispassionate.

To which Vellachi haplessly let out a loud groaning noise and glanced at Kasthuri in commiseration.

What struck him worse was Kasthuri's reclusiveness.

"It's indeed a queenly disposition." Kodanddi couldn't but notice it. "We have to pay the lease paddy too."

"Lease paddy. What is it?" Kasthuri said.

Kodanddi glanced at her. She smiled. He could not smile. He felt shy. Then he explained, "It is the share of harvest given to the landlord by the tenant."

"Oh!" She nodded her head, moving a little making sure her scapular was in the right position, but the two pomegranates refused to succumb.

"Let's call a score of men to accompany her," Kodanddi said to his mother and left the *chayippu*. His footsteps sounded stern and firm, leaving Kasthuri's life on hold. But she had made up her mind to face whatever happened, for men made decisions and women followed.

Yet she valued his character, which was most civilised. Though an illiterate, he never looked at her with bad intentions.

She had even expected inhuman behaviour from them, something wildly voracious. Vellachi, his mother also behaved well, though she had an eye on making her an in-law, for which she couldn't be blamed.

She was grateful to them not only for their nurturing and treatment, but also teaching her the lesson of self-reliance.

She would have been no more if he hadn't spotted her in the woods. For months they nurtured her well, giving what they had and looking after her like a princess.

When he came again to the *chayippu*, Kasthuri said to him, "I'm ready to act as you direct."

He didn't say anything but gently hummed. "… *m*… *m*… *m*." The decision seemed to pain him too, though he had been training his mind for months.

She was sure that they wouldn't accept her. But she wouldn't want to cling on and she knew for certain why she had been left in the woods to die. Either she was to give in to the lechery of the Mannanar, or face his fury.

She was ready to face the fury of the Mannanar if she got a

chance to prove the inquisition wrong. But it would be the rarest of the rare if she continued her stay on the hillock.

The Mannanar had worked out his vendetta when she fell ill, ordering her dumping in the woods.

"Would the Kotta accept me?" she asked herself.

"No," her conscience whispered. Yet she was ready to follow her saviour's instructions.

Vellachi had in the meantime collected the carpel of the jackfruit, removing the rind she placed it in front of her in a spathe of the Areca palm. The sweet aroma tempted her, and she began to munch the carpel. She had never eaten such a sweet '*Thenvarikka*'.[29]

Sitting beside Kasthuri on the pandanus leaf mat woven by her, spread over the cot, Vellachi caressed her and told her not to be distressed.

"Kodanddi is always straightforward. He won't move along the twisted path," Vellachi began to praise her son's features.

Munching the carpel she said that she knew during a period of youthful follies he had been leading the life of folk living in the woods. Yet she liked him. His deeds and expressions showed his overwhelming tender heart.

"We'll set off early in the morning," he said without looking at her for fear that she might be sobbing.

Scores of men and women assembled in the wee hours of the day to accompany them to the Kotta. Some were to carry the paddy, many were to provide security to the Royal lady. They carried swords and bucklers in addition to bows and arrows, and a few were to keep the wild beasts away as they made their way along the deadly wood path. The drummers had their drums on their hips dangling from their necks to the left and were beating

---

[29] A kind of sweet jackfruit.

them. Some carried choppers in their right hands for clearing their path.

When everything was ready, Kodanddi called out Kasthuri, who was in a great hug with Vellachi, both of them in tears.

It was a rare moment, ever memorable or unforgettable. An old black forest dwelling lady lamenting upon the parting of another, though not kin but kin-like – perhaps more. Words stuck in their throats but tears flowed down their cheeks, which were very sincere.

Their hearts almost broke when they parted. Vellachi turned towards the *Olappan kunnu* [30] and prayed to the *Nagakanni*, the goddess deity in the sepulchre that she must return at the earliest.

Vellachi's heart went along with them. She looked at them going out without blinking her eyes till they vanished in the woods. Kasthuri too, looked backward several times. The beating of the drums was heard for a long time, even after they were out of sight.

Looking at the white clouds moving towards the east and at the storks flying away, she stood there stunned all by herself, until the beating of the drums was heard no more. Slowly she went indoors, sad and disheartened and took rest on her cot.

It took several hours to get down to the Kotta. The downhill path seemed more difficult than the uphill. The rocks covered with moss seemed slippery. The wild plants covered the path, which they had to fight their way through.

Men in a line carried the paddy sacks. The beating of the drums and clearing of the way went ahead while Kasthuri stopped at many spots, needing help. Kodanddi did his best to take care of Kasthuri since it would be his responsibility to give her back unharmed, having found her in the woods abandoned.

---

[30] Name of a Hill near the hillock on which the diety of the goddess Nagakanni is situated.

When they were walking down the steep hill, Kodanddi caught hold of her hand and said, "Slowly, the path is slippery, take care."

She felt really secure when he caught hold of her hand. She looked at him. She said, "You hold it tightly, otherwise I may fall."

When she slipped, he caught hold of her, as in an embrace. As she was soft and fragrant as pandanus flowers it was very pleasant. Something in him awakened, but he restrained himself.

She had been in his hut for months and would have been happy if anything had developed as a result.

As they continued down the path, they were shy. But now things seemed different.

She was prettier than ever before. He hadn't noticed her shapely figure before. She was fair complexioned, with soft and smooth skin, fairly round buttocks, two throbbing breasts under the upper garment and above all the princely appearance would be sufficient to move even the most dispassionate.

"Kasthuri," he called out lovingly.

"Kodanddi," she answered, seeping honey.

Then he said, "What will you do if they don't accept you?"

Kasthuri was in a fix, but she said, "I can't anticipate. Let it come whatever it may be. It won't be on the way."

Kodanddi looked at her in amazement. She is a learned woman, he thought. He had never thought of it before.

Then she turned to him and said, "What will you do if they don't accept me?" Now it was his time to be in a fix.

"Where shall I go? Can't you suggest?"

The question darted out right at his heart. In rising perplexity he told her, "It may be your choice."

"My choice!" she exclaimed. Then she said, "I'll keep it in my heart."

Having come to the foot of the steep hill the party was taking rest by the side of a rivulet. They sat on the sacks of paddy which were placed on the rocks. The bowmen placed their bows and arrows nearby. They quenched their thirst from the rivulet and ate flattened rice cake with jaggery, which Vellachi had lovingly given them, for she knew for certain that they would need it on the way.

They resumed as they had to return before dark. The woods seemed thicker and darker. The land being plain and the slope being less, the walk was quite easy, but actually it was precarious for they saw many reptiles and so many wild animals.

Kodanddi said to them to take a staff each so that it could be struck in front of them while they walked to keep the reptiles away.

The wolves roamed about and chased after the wild goats which came on their way. Monkeys made faces at them and jumped from tree to tree with much energy, and swang on the delicate branches of trees.

Kasthuri gazed at them in amazement, but those assorted sights which scared and thrilled her, meant nothing or were very common to others, and had lost interest in them.

Kodanddi made her hurry up as he knew that spot was somewhat precarious.

A leopard was climbing a tree in search of eggs in the bird's nests. Each and every nest was examined with its paw and caused terror to the hatching birds, and the parent ones which flew away wailing.

Wild cats were common, but the sight was rare and astonishing. They looked at them in bewilderment. The bowmen were ready to shoot at it if needed, and tightened the bridles.

The woods were thick, and the air was cool and serene. There was no dust at all, but humidity was high. They didn't feel tired though they had walked a long distance. The warbling of the birds and the music of the mountain spring accompanied them in their mission.

Leeches were very common in the area which stung their legs and sucked blood. They had crawled on even to their private areas, feasted on blood and let themselves down to the ground on their satisfaction. Some of the party men applied a pinch of salt or a piece of tobacco to sever the leeches from their bites.

Kasthuri felt unbearable itching in her groin; she pulled the leech off, blood oozed, and she screamed.

"What?" Kodanddi asked eagerly.

"Leech," she said screaming.

He reached for her. Blood was oozing out from her groin and was trickling down her left thigh to her foot.

Kodanddi plucked some leaves of Pacha chedy, squeezed them on his palm and gave them to her to blot the crevice, which made her scream aloud, which alerted others in the party. They came running and assembled around them.

"What happened?" they said in one voice.

"Nothing," he said. "It was only a leech."

"Don't pull it out," said Kothumban. "You use a pinch of salt for severing it."

"It is said that leech bite is good for health," said Kodanddi.

"Oh! How is that?" she said.

"It sucks the impurities in the blood and purifies it," he explained.

"So leeches are rheumatic physicians?" she mocked him as the pain subsided; she smiled beautifully at him.

"It's believed like that," he said. His words sounded rude but didn't hurt at all.

"Leech is leech," she said ironically. She liked to see his haughtiness.

Far behind the hills, the huge block of black rain clouds moved towards the west as it was the north eastern monsoon going to begin. Suddenly it became so dark that they couldn't move an inch forward.

The thick woods rarely let the sun's rays through, and that too was blocked by the rain clouds. The darkness stranded them in the woods. They couldn't see each other's faces.

They stood in the middle of the woods, amidst the reptiles and wild beasts in the pitch dark.

Kodanddi told them to stand still, like statues, till the light came back.

How long they stood there, perhaps nobody knows, but they heard the reptiles moving on the dry leaves and shuddered seeing the glowing yellow eyes of wild cats, but nobody moved.

But soon Kasthuri felt faint and leant on Kodanddi. He had no choice but to embrace her to stop her from falling. Seeing nothing, he couldn't make her lie on the ground for fear of reptiles, or stinging of scorpions, or centipedes, which were very common in those lands.

The warmth and fragrance of her body excited him. She got stuck to him. It was a rare moment as one might say, perhaps the rarest in the world.

It was completely dark at midday in the thick woods amidst the harmful creatures; nobody could see they were together.

Slowly her consciousness returned, and she embraced him and kissed his cheek.

All of a sudden, it was spring in his heart; and he was thrilled. "Let's go back, I'm horrified," she said finally.

"We can't run away from the realities, my dear," Kodanddi responded.

"They'll kill me," she said.

"Don't be afraid. Such a thing won't happen," he consoled her.

"Once you saved me. Now you are endangering me," she lamented and snorted through her nose.

Tears trickled down her cheeks, and he wiped them off with his own upper cloth and said, "They daren't even touch a hair on your head. But we will abide by the rules and traditions."

"Who makes the rules?" she asked

"I don't know," was his blunt reply.

"Have you ever thought of this?" she asked.

"No, I'm an ordinary man, a forest dweller." Kodanddi stood so polite and simple but firm on his principles. But actually he has been avoiding such remarks.

The cloud which concealed the sun rendered no rain, moved towards the west and slowly the mist disappeared. The sun's rays permeated into the woods to reach down to the earth.

Now that they could see each other, they resumed their journey with haste. The beating of the drums became swift, along with the throbbing of her heart.

Suddenly the woods came to an end, and they entered a village. Hearing the beating of the drums, the villagers crowded on either side of the track and watched the mysterious procession in astonishment.

The Kotta was well-situated on the bank of a river that was not so wide, but it would be flooded during the rainy season. It was a huge mansion building with an inner courtyard guarded by men with swords, day and night.

Seeing the peculiar procession, the guard informed the Mannanar. He came out to the verandah wearing a turban and sword in a sheath, while the Makkachiyars peeped through the small windows.

"Rajalakshmi. She has come with the Karimbalas to take revenge upon us," said the head Makkachiyar.

"Don't spare her." Another Makkachiyar let out her hatred.

Meanwhile, the procession reached the courtyard just one

step down along the verandah. Kodanddi gestured for the paddy bearers to put the sacks of paddy on the verandah. The others, bearing the bows and arrows, took position in the central part of the courtyard and tightened their bridles. The drummers stood behind.

Mannanar called for his steward, Krishnan Nambiar, who came running and stood before him with a bowed head, wearing a loincloth that he had used as a headgear earlier.

They couldn't hear what the two exchanged, but from the gestures, it became obvious to them that she wouldn't be admitted. Yet Kodanddi and Kasthuri dared to enter the verandah, which provoked the Mannanar.

"Stop there!" roared the Mannanar. Everyone present shuddered.

But Kodanddi advanced forward fearlessly, and after saluting him said boldly to the ruthless Mannanar, who was shaking with anger, "We haven't come to attack you, but to pay the lease and to submit what I had got from the woods."

Mannanar raised his eyes and said, "But she?"

"It is Rajalakshmi, the one you abandoned in the woods," Kodanddi said as calmly as he could.

"Oh, her! How dare she come here again?"

While he said it, Mannanar raised his eyebrows, which took a threatening shape. The Makkachiyars who looked through the windows muttered something.

"For me, there's nowhere else to go," Rajalakshmi fell crying.

But the Mannanar paid no heed to it. "I threw the smoking faggot out, that's all," he said emotionlessly. But his lustful eyes were still surveying her features. Her well-proportioned figure and those two plump breasts, and long sparkling eyes, aroused passions in him. The fair round buttocks and beautiful calves ignited his despicable lust.

The Makkachiyars, who knew his character, began gesturing with wild indignation.

"She has lived several months with the Karimbalas. Yet you allow her to come in?" The Makkachiyars blamed him.

He said, "I'm the Mannanar. I have to pay attention to everyone." He wanted to conceal his real intention with a logical argument.

"Then you take in the Karimbalas cast-off." said the head Makkachiyar.

That provoked the Mannanar, who was humiliated and became furious, drew his sword and advanced towards Rajalakshmi to chop off her head.

But before he could do so, Kodanddi leapt in between and shouted angrily, "Hey, Mannanar, look over there." Kodanddi made a war-cry.

Mannanar turned around and saw scores of youths stringing bows and aiming them at him.

He was shocked. He stood as if he was thunder struck.

"Why did you stop? Kill me. You have the right to do so," Rajalakshmi bawled angrily at him.

Rajalakshmi didn't stop.

"Once, you tried to molest me. I protested. You were directed by the Makkachiyars, not by your conscience." She spoke as loud as she could so that everyone in the Kotta could hear her.

"Then you began to hate me. Your hate gradually grew and grew, and you were looking to eliminate me, and when you got the chance, you tried to."

Kodanddi had never heard Rajalakshmi speak so well, and opened his mouth in astonishment.

The Mannanar was in a fix. If he moved forward, the darts would pierce his throat; otherwise he was compelled to listen to her. If he stayed, he would be disgraced. He would become the subject of laughter, not only among the Makkachiyars but even in the streets, he thought.

Neither his mastery in martial arts nor bravery could help him. He retreated to his seat, perplexed.

The Makkachiyars whispered in the inner rooms and spread stories while they cheered the boys of the Kotta who had gone to the *kalaries* nearby to practice their martial arts.

The Young girls hid behind their mothers, putting their fingers in their nostrils and rotating them; and some fondled their budding breasts.

Makkachiyars were eagerly waiting for their husbands to come for their meals.

The vast wealth amassed in the Kotta had permitted them to live lavishly, eat and drink sumptuously and engage in revelries. They had never been under any kind of threat before.

But the situation outside the Kotta was extremely tense. Everybody stood like statues, and nobody spoke.

To ease the situation, the head steward, Krishnan Nambiar, came forward and muttered something into the Mannanar's ear. He sat for a long time, lost in thought.

Finally, the Mannanar got up from his seat and spoke to Kodanddi. It was like an announcement for everyone to hear.

Kodanddi could take Rajalakshmi with him, live happily with her, cultivate as much land as he wanted, be free of tenancy, rear cattle and increase his clan.

Hearing the announcement, the jubilant peasants returned, rejoicing. They took Kodanddi and Kasthuri on their shoulders and beat their drums. The uphill path, usually harder and riskier, seemed much easier today.

The trees in blossom extended floral umbrellas, and the

drizzling rain sprinkled rose water on them. The gentle breeze laden with fragrance and cool rain swept away, making their task easier. The jubilant human voices mixed with the 'Hoi-Hoi' sounds and beating of the drums in the atmosphere of the hillock.

Normally climbing up the mountain would take more time than the downward walk, but today it took only half the time.

Hearing the beating of the drums and the sounds of the jubilant human voices, Vellachi was so excited that she didn't know how to receive them nor knew for certain how things had turned out. So she stood gazing at the blue mountain in bewilderment.

Kodanddi and Kasthuri were given a rousing welcome on the hillock. Like a great fighter after having performed some victorious deeds and receiving a hero's reception in his home town.

Vellachi ran into the house, lit the oil lamp having seven wicks and worshipped. Then, holding the lamp, she led them to an inner room and treated them to fruits and milk.

The others in the party were asked to sit. Vellachi briskly engaged in cooking a feast for them. The rice was put on to boil in a large copper vessel.

Men and women in the party readily went to help her. One began chopping the meat of the deer which Vellachi had bought from a snare hunter, another engaged in preparing suitable roots, another was powdering spices in a wooden mortar, and another frying the pigeon-pea in a large flat earthenware pot for making dessert.

It was decided that the '*Pudamuri*' should be performed late at night on the nearest auspicious day.

Kodanddi and Kasthuri were taking rest in the inner room. They were thinking over the unexpected turn of events. Both had apprehensions about whether she would be content to live with what she got.

Vellachi was so excited and enthusiastic that she spoke to everyone in detail, even a passer-by, about how her son, Kodanddi, was going to marry a princess. When the listeners placed their fingers on their noses in astonishment, she would become angry.

"My son is a prince, a Karimbala prince." Then she would turn away, swishing her buttocks and her breasts swinging.

On the auspicious day when the moon, Venus and Mercury fall in a line, the most auspicious time, it was decided to give *Pudava* to Kasthuri.

Kodanddi and his friends walked a long way to the Saliya streets to get the bridal *pudava* and new clothes for close relatives.

Though it seemed simple, much hard work and energy were needed to make the arrangements.

Kothumban and other youths, on the very next day, began to make the *pandal* (barn) for which they collected a good number of Palmyra leaves and bamboo pillars, found in abundance in that part of the landscape; several groups of men and women were fully engaged, some were sent out to invite family and friends while others were fully duty bound on the hillock.

A large quantity of paddy was stewed and dried in the sun. Several women were engaged in pounding the paddy in large wooden mortars.

Dhal-gram was cleaned and dehydrated in a large flat circular dish and was stored ready to prepare food. Dehydrated green gram was peeled and finely separated for dessert using large grind stones and heavy pestles.

Vellachi was everywhere, always chattering, giving instructions to everyone as if some great festival on going.

When completed, the barn, not too big nor too small, looked like a green carpet raised on bamboo pillars. The ground was levelled and smeared with cow dung. Several mats were laid out on the platform so that the guests could take rest or sleep.

The much-awaited auspicious day came. Men, women and children began to arrive at the hillock of Kudiyatti before noon.

Vellachi and Kodanddi received them, led them to the pandal adorned with decorative leaves, and served them food and drink. In addition to palm toddy, there was a large stock of hootch, the tribe's favourite.

By the end of the day, the hillock of Kudiyatti had witnessed a large turnout of people.

Everything was arranged. A ceremonial lamp was lit at one side of the *pandal*. Hundreds of lamps of *hydnocarpus pentandra* made it a palace of stars when looked at from afar or a galaxy of stars from even farther away.

Men and women thronged to the barn, making it full to the brim, and engaged in talking or chewing pan.

When the auspicious time drew near, the old and venerable head of the clan brought the bride and bridegroom to the barn and made them sit in front of the ceremonial lamp. At the prescribed time, Kodanddi gave the *pudava* to Kasthuri, the men cheered, and the women made the sound of the *'kurava'*.

After the ceremony, everyone rushed to quench their thirst and hunger while others waited hungrily for their turn.

It was early morning when the festivities came to an end. The bride and the bridegroom had bathed themselves in the rivulet before they entered the bridal chamber. It was believed that immense cosmic energy is released on the earth during the early hours of the day. Fertilization at this auspicious time would yield sons capable of becoming Emperors.

In the bridal chamber, they sat for a long time looking at each other, not talking, perhaps thinking over the unexpected turn of events.

Though from the outside, they differed greatly, inwardly,

they matched perfectly. For her, he was the saviour and protector, and she sincerely bonded with him.

She was the princess in high esteem for him, though she fell prey to conspirators and powermongers.

A mutual respect made a strong bond, and love acted as the '*Ashtabandham*'.[31]

Perhaps she would have lived in pomp and splendour, and would have lived like a queen in the palace amidst prosperity and luxury. But ill fate had befallen her; and she was dumped in the woods as waste, Kasthuri thought. She took a deep breath.

As the darkness increased, the light of the lamp became dimmer. Soon it was blown out by the cold wind. And in the cloudy dark wee hours of the day, they shared the sweet moments of their life.

Kodanddi left his bed as usual to go to his farmland, an unerring practice since his youth, from which nothing could deter him. The secret of his success lay in his observance of this routine, but that day he wished Kasthuri was with him.

Suddenly he smelt the fragrance of pandanus. He turned round and was astonished to see Kasthuri behind a yam in the early hour of the day, drenched in mist. She smiled. It was so beautiful, as the moonlight in the winter.

Slowly they came nearer and hugged. He could feel the heat of her passions. Those two fleshy breasts, not cool but warm, pressed on his own chest. He moved his fingers through her hair, kissing her cheeks incessantly. Slowly his hands lowered, massaging every inch of her body, arousing both of them. Not only their loins but their whole body throbbed wildly. They writhed and wriggled with the pangs of passion. He didn't say anything, and neither did she.

---

[31] The cement usually used to install deities in temples.

The moonlight spread the mattress adorned with jasmine and petals of roses. The mist sprayed rosewater on them, and the vegetable garden became their bridal chamber. The heat of passion evaporated the cool dew dropped over them by the heaven of love.

Before the first rays of day break, smeared with sweat and mud, they staggered to the rivulet for a dip in the water and walked home, the sweet languor still clinging to them.

Vellachi was waiting for them with ginger coffee. Smiling frequently, she welcomed them. Not looking at her, they went in. Kasthuri seemed ashamed, looking at her through the corner of her eyes.

For a moment, Vellachi thought of her own experiences with Chavanian in the woods. Setting off in search of tubers and digging deep for them, having their revelry in the meantime.

"Oh! What exciting days those were!" she said to herself.

Eating wild tubers and meat and drinking wild honey while having their revelries day and night, everywhere in the woods, in the barns and in the rivulets.

The memory itself had the power of thrilling her.

They sipped ginger coffee along with mother's love. Then they took a rest.

When they got up, so many people had come to see their '*Thamburatty Kutty*.' She went to the rivulet to refresh herself before making an appearance for them. The sweet langour still clung to her.

The crystal-clear water trickled down to the store pit, filling the pond enough for her to dip her whole body in to cool the heat of passion. The bark of *Acacia Intsia* cleansed her body. Pandanus flowers made it fragrant.

Adept and enthusiastic, she smiled contentedly. The

successful culmination made her sip in the enjoyment of marital love, which was far beyond her expectations, for she had never thought of him to be so powerful and passionate.

Dressing, she looked like a princess. The women folk surrounded her; looking at her and touching her.

As she smiled gracefully, the women and children were enchanted by her charisma.

Chapter 4

Scores of women and children were lined up to see their 'Thamburatty Kutty'. Women with uncovered breasts and naked children but, of course, not with dishevelled hair and running noses, eagerly waited for her. There were none too old or too young.

The women filled their spare time in mudslinging while the young girls fondled their flower buds or inserted their fingers in their thrilling spots. Their mothers intimidated them with their probing eyes.

Vellachi gave them salted gooseberries and mangoes. Children ate them with great appetite, and women gulped saliva down.

Kasthuri didn't express any discontent towards them though the children looked ugly and smelt foul as though they were her subjects – having equal rights. Some children touched her feet, but she forbid them, saying, "I'm one among you."

"But here, everyone says you are a *Thamburatty*." A young girl remarked, raising her eyebrows.

"How is that possible?" Kasthuri said to her. Then she explained, "Thamburatty is at the *Kovilakam*, and I'm here."

"It's right. Now your Majesty is here," the girls said politely.

"Where was your Majesty a year ago?" the young girl said.

Kasthuri was in a fix. The women and girls looked at each other. But they were listening to her.

"You may have heard so many fanciful stories," she said to

them with a smile and looked at them through the corner of her eyes.

"You needn't try to deceive us," they said in one voice.

It seemed that they were determined to find the truth, and further, she couldn't turn a deaf ear to those simple, innocent queries.

Kasthuri thought that she needn't hide her story from them. Instead, it should be rolled out before them.

"I'm the only granddaughter to the Raja. My childhood was so happy that you can't even believe it. My mother died during delivery, and the King, my grandfather, appointed seven ladies to attend to me. Hence, I got seven mothers instead of one. In fact, they were competing with each other to take care of me. The ministers and stewards looked at me with the utmost respect, and I enjoyed all the royal pleasures at a very early age. Like a butterfly in a colourful garden, I flew from one flower to another." She paused for a moment.

"Didn't you get schooling?" the girl said while wiping away mucus with the corner of her sleeve.

"Of course. My tutoring was at home. My tutors taught me well in case one day I would become the queen. All this went well till the King met with an accident."

"What was it?" the girls said, raising their concern.

"It was nothing but a slip." Kasthuri sighed deeply. She took a pause and had a far-off look in her eyes. Tears trickled down her cheeks and wet her top. She wiped her eyes with her sleeve. Her face became as red as cherry fruit. It seemed that she would weep.

"Don't be so sad, *Thamburatty.*" The girls consoled her. Then they said, "Kodanddiyettan is a very good man. He'll look after you like a queen."

"It's a secret plot," she said.

"What?"

"A secret plot – a conspiracy on the Raja's life to eliminate him," she explained.

"For what?"

"To capture power, why else?"

"Power? We don't understand." They didn't want to conceal their ignorance.

"I'll explain," she said. "It's some kind of strength. If I lift that grindstone," pointing to the grindstone, she said, "I'll have the power to lift it. Likewise, Raja has the power to rule the country," she said with a sigh.

"Can *the* Raja lift the country?" The girl's ignorance aroused laughter, but Kasthuri liked it.

"Ruling is not lifting or carrying," she said, smiling. "It's controlling the people with his might."

"Can't you rule the country if you have become the queen?" the girl said.

Like a javelin, the query went right into her heart, penetrating her. She took a deep breath yet managed to stay calm and composed.

"I have a cousin," she resumed her story. "She's the daughter of my grandfather's youngest sister. After her mother's demise, she lived with us. Grandfather brought us both up together and alike, without any discrimination. But being crooked and selfish, she hatched a plot against my grandfather and me. Constantly in touch with the minister and chief of the army, she had conspired against us."

"What is her name?" was the girl's query.

"Vasundhara, Vasundhara Devi is her full name. But people used to call her 'Vasuki', the great serpent. Her poisonous tongue first turned against me in the form of scandals!"

The girl's eyes seemed unbelieving, and Kasthuri paused for a while, allowing them to digest what they had heard.

"Having entrusted the affairs of the state to the minister and chief of the army, grandfather was fully engaged in the welfare department. So, the people liked him; they trusted him and loved him. Yet the powermongers were looking for a chance to destabilise him. He would wake up at four in the morning. Having performed his ablutions, he would practice martial arts for at least an hour. Being the best archer, even in his sixties, no one dared to challenge him. He visited the lord Krishna temple at six in the morning every day. He was devoted to Krishna and bowed his head before none other than Him.

"On that fateful day, the King slipped from the staircase and fell, hitting his back on the edge of the steps and fracturing his backbone, compelling him to stay in bed for a long period. It was found out only later that the King had slipped from the stair owing to the secret plot hatched by Vasundhara.

"She might be hanged," the girls burst out with anger. They were innocent as lambs.

"It might be so if I had power," Kasthuri said. "The minister and chief of the army tried to avoid me, consulting all matters with Vasundhara. They never came to me, dutifully engaged in the service of my grandfather, the King. Externally everything was right, and nobody had the slightest hint about the conspiracy. They even pretended to bow before me whenever they met me in the corridors of power. Days and months passed by, and seasons changed, but no signs of improvement in his health were found. Slowly but surely, the king lost his power of speech too. The injury caused to his backbone had completely paralysed him.

"Vasundhara became more powerful, and the three ruled the state, side lining me. But the people visited me whenever they came to the palace to see their once beloved King. I was the only heir for them; this they knew for certain. The news that the King was confined to bed spread far and wide, and people came in large numbers. The three might have conspired for my execution, and they were looking at finding low tricks to accomplish this paid attention to me before they left the palace…"

"Why had she hatched so much hatred towards you?"

"The hatred towards me was woven in her own loom. She would have thought that after the demise of the King, naturally, I would become the queen. The very thought sprouted envy in her heart. The minister and chief of the army fertilised that envy, and let it grow to a vile demon. She was waiting for a chance."

"Hadn't she tried to kill you?" the girl asked.

"No, she hadn't, because she was intelligent and clever. You know people loved the King, so me too. Being his darling, they showed that love towards me; she dared not kill me. The people would turn against her if she did it."

"Then, how did it happen you were expelled?" was her query.

"The Raja had become almost deaf and dumb due to the fall. He uttered meaningless words, which were misinterpreted by the three as they wanted. Since they were the words of the Raja, nobody could deny them at all, and this created a situation congenial for exploitation."

"Allegations?"

"Of course, but fake. They alleged that I had a secret alliance with a youth belonging to a lower caste, but I hadn't. A youth used to visit me with fresh *Kurikkoottu*[32] and cosmetics every morning. He was so sincere and punctual in his duty, a friendship slowly developed between us. Nothing more than that, but they spread scandals against me, that we had physical contact. I attended to my grandfather and performed my duties as usual as

---

[32] Sandalwood paste and saffron for making the caste mark on the forehead.

though nothing happened. Everyone who knew me knew that there was not even a trace of truth in it. But the rumour spread faster than a storm inside the palace and across the country, as they intended.

"Man can stop fire with water, river by building a dam across it, but not hearsay, since it has no origin. The people who lamented upon the fall of their beloved King heard those stale words and thought it a furuncle upon the hunchback. As usual on that cursed day, he came with the '*Kurikkoottu*' and entered my Harem (chamber). As he was about to leave, the door was shut from outside, and we two were confined in the '*Harem*[33]' for a long time. He knocked on the door from inside, but it did not open; only then did it come into my head that it was done with bad intentions.

"He sat at the threshold and I on a chair. He was afraid to speak, but not I. The minutes were endless, and we eagerly waited for the door to be opened. He was shivering with fear and exhaustion. I tried to console him, saying that nothing would happen. But he fell down exhausted. I made him lie on the 'Diwane', gave him water to drink and fanned him. All of a sudden the door was unlocked, and many people rushed in. They were to see the scene, the princess fanning a servant boy. There were many, including the minister, the chief of the army and the inquisitor whom I knew was a sycophant of Vasundhara. One of them came forward and asked whether they had interrupted anything. Enraged with anger, I slapped his face and the team left the 'harem'. While they were leaving, the inquisitor announced that I would have to face the inquisition. Perhaps they would have faced the heat of my fury for the first time.

"To gain positions, some people rub the shoes of the rulers,

---

[33] Chamber.

and some others lick. I smelt a rat during their visit. The inquisition would be done soon. They would say that they had the consent of my grandfather, the King. How the consent had been given would remain a mystery forever. It seemed to me that they had designed their secret plot very easily and brought it into force stage by stage.

"'What had I done against them?' my conscience asked me.

"Many had secretly said to me, 'Why can't you protest?' It shook me vigorously.

"'A rebellion?' The prompting became hard to bear. Several chieftains had the same opinion. But I couldn't bear to think of it because my grandfather was the King, even though it was only in name. I couldn't think of leading a revolt against my grandfather, who had been lying in bed for so long.

"I was perplexed. Life was staring at me. Nobody visited me that day though I yearned for it. Being alone and unattended, I felt completely dejected. I called for my attendants, but none could be seen in my vicinity. Then I went to visit my grandfather. The corridor, once the centre of power, was empty; now her lobby was busy with pomp and splendour. When I walked into the corridor, some people saw me, but they turned their faces away from me. I felt it like a slap on my face. Some looked at me with contempt, and some secretly gossiped. When I walked into the chamber, the attendants walked out without a greeting; perhaps for the first time.

"Grandfather looked at me with bulging eyes. Unable to speak, he seemed to be overwhelmed with feelings, and tears rolled down his hollow face. He wanted to say many things to me, but words couldn't come out as though they had been obstructed in his throat. He struggled hard to overcome the affliction, but still he couldn't. I lost control. The scene could have melted even a hard-hearted man. How could I remain dispassionate? Though overwhelming compassion was forbidden during the visits to him, I went to him, embraced him and wiped off his tears with the corner of my sleeve. It was an unforgettable touching hug between the brave King and his beloved granddaughter, loving and compassionate. His attendants requested that I leave him alone to provide him peace of mind.

"With a heavy heart, I returned to my chamber, threw myself on the bed. I remained like the whole day and night until the tears washed away the wound in my heart. Spreading rumours was part of alienating me from the people. Whether people believed them or not, it was natural that, there would be an erosion in the public reputation about me. It was what happened to me. People used to visit me earlier whenever they came to the palace. Those good days were gone, and my countdown had begun. I thought that my head would be chopped off by the knights or I would be sent to the Aramana. The Mannanar Kotta came to my awareness, where the Makkachiyars would be my companions and the Mannanar, my King.

"I yearned earnestly that the former would be better. Living dishonoured was a thousand times worse than death. But accepting it on one's own would be a great sin against His wish and the devastation of the holiness earned by the virtuous deeds of several births. The public support I had gathered was deteriorating heavily as the royal secret had become the talk of the town. For several months they completely cut off my rapport with the people. But the fire had gone deep in, and couldn't be rooted out until their hearts were pulled off.

"Vasundhara had begun the preparations for the inquisition secretly for which she could gain the consent of the King. How she obtained it, I didn't know. Perhaps the King might have been misconstrued, which could be easier in those days. Oh! I have forgotten myself," Kasthuri said, raising her eyes. Then she said, "You got bored?"

"No." The girls were defiant. In fact, they were eagerly listening to her.

She had become so enthusiastic as if she had been devoid of cold when submerged fully in the river. The sweet langour still clung to her. Yet she tried to recollect the chain of events.

"Where did I stop?" she asked.

"You stopped at the inquisition," said the girls all together. They were keen on remembering what they had heard.

"What's inquisition?" The girls didn't grasp the idea. They were looking at each other in amazement.

"It's a kind of trial," she said.

"By who?" The girls were eager to know.

"Of the King's choice," was her reply.

"But the King?"

"The King was lying in bed. Somehow, they had secured his consent. Nobody seemed to know how they did it, but surely not by fair means but by foul and evil designs. They were four, all men of her choice, prejudiced and partial. Having sat elegantly in the courtroom, they summoned me. I appeared before them without any hesitation or inductiveness because I had nothing to hide, but they seemed prejudiced and determined. I was asked to sit when I entered the courtroom and the trial began. It all seemed an absurd drama. The inquisitor ordered the main witness to be called. A man appeared and stood with his head bowed in front of the inquisitor. He didn't look at me, but his face was familiar to me. I remembered well. He was an ardent supporter of Vasundhara. He was her right-hand man.

"When the inquisitor ordered him to narrate what had

happened, he told the court that he had found me and a youth in a compromising position. When I tried to question him, the inquisitor stopped me, saying I would get a chance to explain later. When asked why the door had been locked from outside, he told the court that it was for taking us into custody red-handed and bringing us before the court. There were three more witnesses too. All of them turned out to be the same chip. I was completely taken aback and knew for certain that it was all to get me evicted from the palace. All four witnesses danced to Vasuki's tune.

"The inquisitor finally asked me what I had to say. At first, I was reluctant to explain. Something seemed to block my throat; words would not come. Yet I thought if I didn't respond, the inquisitor might think that the guilt had restrained me from doing so and that I had been deceiving the people by adulterating the high place. The princess whom they believed to be the number one fell from a high state. They would throw fate where everyone found comfort for their misdeeds.

"The inquisitors were waiting for my response. If I didn't speak, a wrongdoing would have been left unquestioned, and history would blame me. So I burst out at them, questioning their power for inquisition, reminding them of the risk they would be taking throughout their life. But the inquisitors were adamant, saying they were bound to their duty, and I could plead to the higher office if I felt it inappropriate or unjust.

"Abruptly, they stopped and rose up. I knew it was a prejudiced inquisition that nobody could alter. Certainly, I waited for the decision, for it began to make the heat of hatred unbearable. I returned to my harem, which seemed to grin at me, and I felt embarrassed. Vasundhara had cleverly pulled the rug from under me, charmed the minister and chief of the army and finally, the King. She might have been playing the tricks since his great fall, to bring everyone under her spell.

"Waiting for the decision, I spent three more days without eating. Sleep had been a forbidden fruit to me. Late at night on the third day, everything belonging to me was loaded on a cart, and I was cast off to the Kotta with three attendants. Two were men and one was a woman. The woman attendant took rest inside the kotta. They were instructed to dump me at the Kotta with my belongings and return immediately. That night expedition I will never forget. Nobody dared to question the decision of the inquisitor.

"The cart moved slowly, shaking and making a 'Ghana-Ghana' sound as it went. I sat on the platform, stretching my legs and leaning on the cart's side, covering my body with a woollen cloth. The cart driver steered it while making 'Hoi-Hoi' sounds but never whipped his bullocks – because they were young and smart and didn't need that sort of prompting.

"My attendants whispered all the way. The 'Ghana-Ghana' and 'Hoi-Hoi' sounds continued as we advanced forward in the light of the lantern. I was in a turmoil. I knew for certain that the days awaiting me wouldn't be so peaceful and happy for me but would prick and pierce my heart. When half of the distance was covered, we halted so that the bullocks could take some rest. The cart driver gave his bullocks some hay and led them to a stream nearby. Then he allowed his bullocks to rest for a while. The attendants and the cart driver talked to each other in low voices, but they were reluctant to talk to me, which might have been because of fear or respect, but more likely was due to contempt. They might have been saying what a pathetic fall it was while keeping their fingers on their noses.

"The cool gentle breeze pacified our fatigue, and the moon appeared in the sky with a little shyness, yet it was bright. The moon in the winter looked so beautiful. The mist added its beauty. The trees and plants, all drenched in the mist, swayed in the breeze and bid me goodbye. It all looked like a shadow drama where the characters played behind the screen. Vasundhara would have played well behind the curtain if she were present, since she is crooked.

"'Thamburatty, would you like a drink of water?' my maid said to me.

"'Yeah, I feel thirsty and hungry,' I said. 'Actually, my stomach has been growling for days.'

"She gave me rice cake and water, and I ate voraciously as though I hadn't had any food for days, and I drank a lot of water. Yet it couldn't satisfy the hunger in my stomach. If Vasundhara were there, I wouldn't hesitate to eat her raw. We resumed our night journey. The oxen being sleepy and fatigued, were reluctant. Further, the bumpy road made the going hard, and I felt that my backbone would be crushed to pieces by the time we reached our destination. We moved ahead by the light of the lantern, swaying and swinging on the slushy, muddy road. The sound of the cart's wheels echoed through the hills on either side.

"I lay on a bundle of clothes which made me feel somewhat better. I looked outside. In the early hours of the day, the hills appeared blue and stood like a security wall touching the sky. The crowing of a cock marked the beginning of the day. People were awakened. The oil lamps were lit in people's houses. Men and women were at work. Women ignited fires at the hearths and began preparing the food for the day. They had begun it earlier because they had to work in the paddy fields or farms of landlords from dawn to dusk. The men were engaged in the cleaning of their cow sheds or milking. Everyone except those who were confined to bed and little ones were active.

"The early rays of the rising sun had begun to paint the

eastern horizon, and its magnificence made me fancy the golden days of my childhood. But suddenly, the day came alive of its own free will, letting out not only humans but all the living beings on earth as well. Naturally, I had to cope with the reality. The Ghana-Ghana sound of the wheels of the cart and Hoi-Hoi sound of the cart driver aroused the people. Women peeped through their windows and came out. We are nearing the Kotta. The women and children flocked on either side of the street to spectate the mighty procession. They were eager to know who was in the cart and were astonished to hear it was the princess who was to be dumped to become the Makkachiyar."

"'What fate has brought her here?' they asked.

"'Her mischief, what else!' someone answered. 'But that won't stop here,' he added.

"Others laughed, yet they came out to see the distinguished outcast. Finally, we reached the door of the Mannanar Kotta. It was closed, and two men with swords guarded it. Hearing the noise, a good number of people gathered at the door. The door was opened, and two security men rushed out of the door. Raising their eyebrows, they looked at the driver. The cart driver handed over the majestic letter to one of the security men. At once, he returned to hand it over to the Mannanar.

"Knowing the majestic importance, he himself came out to receive me, but he was taken aback seeing me stepping down, for he had expected me to be on the throne after the incumbent. He remembered the rumour which had been spreading in the inner circles of the palace a few months ago but hadn't ever dreamed this would happen. Slowly the residents came out, one by one. Mostly, they were Makkachiyars with uncovered breasts, their once paramours turned legal, and their sons and daughters with princely looks, attended by servants and butlers. Guards and army men of the Mannanar numbered twenty, all proficient in martial arts.

"Standing in the middle of the courtyard, I had a glimpse of the Kotta, which looked like Ettukettu or two Nalukettu joined together by a narrow passage. The walls were built with red laterites, not plastered, of course, but polished well. The tiled roof, cow dung smeared floor, and old and new building structures coming together to give it a grand aristocratic style. The senior Makkachiyar received me, holding my hand, and took me inside. The servants brought my luggage in. I went in to refresh myself in the bathroom, having no choice nor chance for protest. The icy cold water washed away my fatigue. Having refreshed myself, I moved straight to the room allotted to me.

"It usually took a long time to dry my hair, but that day it dried quickly, which might have been due to the heat of my head. Then I went for a nap lying down on the divan. Having left the oxen to graze, the cart driver and the two assistants also rested at the corner of the long verandah. They felt hungry and thirsty. They had already planned to return soon after the midday meal.

"It began to annoy me that I was ousted without the slightest protest. No one dared to raise his voice against the sheer injustice done to me.

"'Did I put up a protest?' I asked myself.

"'No,' my conscience answered quickly.

"'Then, how could I blame others?' I said to myself. 'The ousting was planned so thoroughly that no one could find any loopholes.'

"No one tried to find the truth, and everyone believed Vasundhara. The inquisitor was dancing to her tune. Earlier I had the support of the people, which she purposefully stopped by spreading hearsay. She had incapacitated my grandfather, taken over his powers one by one, and talked so well that everyone who could hear her would be charmed. She shed crocodile tears over the fall of the King, her uncle, and she won over the people."

"Was it a killing by licking?" The girl who was so silent all this time asked.

"Yeah, as true as sunlight," Khasthuri said to her. "I bid my assistants goodbye as they finished their lunch, and they drove off. I felt I would vomit, and I had a severe headache. I lay in the divan. The Makkachiyars and their children gathered around me. They wanted to touch me to feel the softness of my skin, and children pulled my hair to test whether it was real. Someone wanted to find out whether my cloth was silk or pure cotton. I told them that I was feeling unwell and would like to take rest. Soon they left the place, and I was alone. The senior Makkachiyar came. She had very large buttocks, breasts not so droopy and lips red from chewing betel. She seemed to be the steward for the Mannanar. Taking my hand in hers, she babbled lovingly but sometimes splashed the red fluid from her mouth without apology. Her eyes were large and black, and her cheeks robust. She had thick black curly hair. Her lustful eyes seemed to be capable of causing arousal in the minds of men, even in her fifties. She trotted away to the kitchen gracefully like a swan saying she would return to me in the afternoon.

"Lunch, usually a hearty meal, would be served sumptuously. Par boiled rice with a wild meat dish, usually wild boar or wild goat or deer. Sometimes the antlers would be there because if the hunted animal was killed under the jurisdiction of the Mannanar, it would be brought to the Aramana, and the right back thigh, including the posterior and the head of the hunted animal, would be cut and submitted to the Mannanar as the landlord's share. Every day there would be several hunting groups, and so meat was abundant in the Aramana.

"'What will I do if meat is served to me?' I asked myself.

"Up to that day, I hadn't tasted meat. If I refused it, a problem would arise, and I would be more alienated. But if I accepted it, the purity gained through so many years of abstinence would be lost. So I was in a fix.

"When the meat was served, I didn't want to cause any problems, so I chose to be content with what I had, and I ate it. At first, it was difficult for me to eat the meat, which made me vomit. Slowly but surely, I got used to the taste of the wild meat, and I was able to eat it without vomiting. Since then, meals without meat would be like forcing me to drink bitter medicine. Months and seasons passed by, and life seemed to be quite easy without stress at first. Eating wild meat every day fattened my cheek. Made my body fatter and my skin reddish. I began to spend more time looking at the mirror and felt that I had become more beautiful. The Mannanar, though in his middle age, began to look at me, first in private and then openly, which irritated me. The Head Makkachiyar had warned me about his lustful ways. I hadn't paid any heed to this; he seemed not so courageous to approach me, and act on his lust.

"But he managed to get many girls in a snare, and his revelry continued profoundly. He always wanted new and young though his Makkachiyar mellowed him at night. Whenever he met me, he would look at me longingly. No one dared to resist him as he had the power to bless or kill. Women inside wondered in private what made his manhood so powerful. I had heard them whispering.

"'He eats a whole wild goat at a sitting,' one of the Makkachiyars said.

"'That is why he is a ram,' another had opined.

"'Now his mind is on her,' the former had said.

"'Who?' the older had said with a sense of loss.

"'Rajalakshmi,' the former had said emotionlessly.

"'Then, he will know she is a princess,' the latter had said.

"'But an outcast,' the former had said.

"'They fabricated stories to push her out,' the head Makkachiyar had said piteously.

"'How do you know that?' the other Makkachiyar was sceptical of the claim.

"'Only the bedfellows know the intensity of the night fever,' the head Makkachiyar said.

"Others gave a dubious glance at her. The swan walked away slowly, and others dispersed. He had become blind with lust, and I had to be careful. So I was in a trap. I had understood. I decided to be careful and I bolted the doors of my room even in daytime and tried to keep away from his eyes as much as possible. Yet sometimes, I would accidentally step right in front of him, only to become a pleasure to his eye. Often he would appear as a dandy. Though a libertine, the Mannanar had his vacillations. Whether I would surrender or not, whether to approach me, or make me surrender by other means. The cat waited for the mouse to turn up but was scared because it was not an ordinary mouse, he flagged mostly.

"'She will give in one day,' the libertine had murmured, smacking the saliva accumulated in his mouth.

"His stewards had come to report to him about the tenants and tax payments. The harvest was ruined by the unprecedented heavy rain, and the farmers suffered a heavy blow that affected the tax payments. The adverse weather had mutilated their dreams. Humiliated by the returns, some were forced to flee, the Mannanar was told. Several farmers were on the verge of suicide owing to the huge loss, and their landlord didn't consider their expenses. The hard workers supplied them with the things they needed. The weavers brought clothes of their choice, earthen vessels were brought by the potters, and smithies gave them tools and ornaments. The grocers provided them with grocery items. The washer man washed their clothes, and barbers cut their hair and shaved them. All were paid after the harvest.

"'Think of the heavy expenditure for running the Aramana,' the Mannanar told his stewards.

"'But what will they do if they don't have any means to pay?' they asked.

"'We are running twenty-five Kalaries. How much do they need?'

Mannanar looked at them. They didn't say anything but glanced at each other. 'Oh! We understand that. But here…'

"But he could not complete it. The Mannanar's intimidating looks made him swallow the rest. 'How dare you counter me?' Mannanar grinned. Nobody spoke after that.

"The mid-noon had passed by. The Mannanar had asked stewards to stay for lunch. They took their lunch and went out belching. I had underscored him as a lecher. But having heard his interactions with his stewards, I came to know that he was an efficient ruler. He being a master of martial arts; no one dared to counter him. The common man was afraid of him. For the protection of the people and for keeping law and order under control, the skilled men from the kalaries were always helpful to him. But the aristocrats had hatred in them, not because of his lechery or inefficiency but because of his inferior caste. They waited for a chance, keeping their deceit in abeyance but, of course, dared not openly revolt.

"The Mannanar usually picked up young and beautiful maids from the neighbourhoods and kept them in the Aramana for years as assistants till their marriages. The poor peasants had a liking for it, not knowing the full extent of the trap. The atmosphere was calm and serene, and life in the Aramana seemed happier. The residents ate and drank sumptuously. The men practised archery in the *kalari* in the mornings, fencing with sticks, swords and *urumi* till it became too hot, swam in the river in the evenings and slept with the Makkachiyars at Night, bothering about nothing. Life was peaceful and beautiful to them, but I was a caged parrot, got everything supplied but kept apart from its flock.

"Having learnt the disposition of the Mannanar, it began to develop a kind of rape-phobia in me. I bolted the doors of my room even during the daytime when there was no one other than me. Sometimes the Makkachiyars accompanied me when I went out for a swim or walked to the temple. But I had a feeling that wherever I went, his longing eyes followed me. I had determined to act as a princess if an emergency occurred, whatever the consequences. During the menstruation period, women were shut up in small narrow rooms at the rear and had no freedom to enter the main building or contact others. Food would be supplied in the rooms, and every day the '*Vannathy*'[34] lady took away the putrefied cloth for washing and supplied the '*Mattu*[35]'. As there were so many women residents, the Vannathy had to visit the Aramana every day to take the putrefied cloths contaminated with menstruation fluid. They were to take rest for seven days, and contact with men was forbidden on those days. I thought those days were better as I was emancipated from rape-phobia.

"I slept with the Makkachiyars in those days and came to know more about them. We could open our hearts in the semi-

---

[34] Washer woman.
[35] Substitute cloth.

darkness of the 'Theendari *kolayi*'[36]. Each one had a story of deception, either by the loved one or someone with a blood bond, which wouldn't be revealed, fearing notoriety. Uma, a young Makkachiyar, fell into tears while she told her story to me. She was the only daughter in an orthodox *illam*[37] that owned a vast estate. Being so beautiful and humble, she could beckon the love and attention of everybody. Her father had left her with his cousin when he and his wife went to '*Murajapam*[38]', which lasted for fifty-six days in south Travancore. Like a plum, she had become juicy flesh, stimulating the relative's suppressed passion. He spoilt her and brought ostracism upon her. Her parents breathed their last not long after she had been declared an outcast by the inquisition, and the large estate owned by her father came under the possession of the consummate sinner. Later it was heard that he had seduced her intentionally to gain the vast range of properties.

"Uma had asked me, 'Wasn't it better for him to kill me?'

"'Of course,' I had told her, though it seemed very cruel.

"'But the disgrace wouldn't be washed off,' she had said.

"'It would remain for generations,' I had replied.

"'He would have to pay dearly,' she said emotionlessly, looking into the distance.

"'Of course, with interest,' I said. She had tried to smile. But couldn't cast off the gloom.

"From that day onwards, she had been like a younger sister to me till we parted later. Most of the Makkachiyars had such stories of deception that led them to the Aramana. But a few remained exceptions who wantonly shared the forbidden fruit to

---

[36] place occupied by the menstruated woman.
[37] House of a brahmin.
[38] A ritual for fifty six days in south Travancore.

quench the heat of their passion. I had consoled her and told her that she was not at all guilty. Not revealing my identity, I had embraced her. But she knew for certain where I had come from.

"'My humilitation is meagre when compared to yours,' she said, glancing at me curiously. I hadn't denied her for the fact that if the comparison of loss could alleviate her sorrow, then let it be. But she had lost her chastity, an irreparable loss forever, which led her eventually into the confines of the Aramana. I felt pity for her, spoke to her and wiped off her tears.

"Then she asked me, 'How can you bear your loss so dispassionately?'

I raised my eyebrows as if to ask, 'Who told you?'

"'No one,' she denied by gestures.

"'Then?'

"'Are you a recluse?' Uma asked.

"'No, I'm as human as you with flesh and blood.' I said seriously.

"'Then, how did it happen for you to be expelled?' she too became serious.

"'It's all because of greed,' I said.

"'Greed for what?' she asked in her ignorance.

I didn't want to answer her directly. 'Who's the most powerful person in this country?' I asked her.

"'The King. Who else?' she said.

"'Then who else does want not to become a king? For at least once in life?' I posed to her.

"'Nobody,' she admitted my views.

"'Usually, the eldest son of the King ascends the throne after his demise,' I began to explain. 'But if there are no sons, the King's daughter wears the crown. Suppose the King is alive, and he has no sons but has a niece. His only daughter dies at an early younger age had left her daughter behind, a grand daughter to the King. Who has the rightful claim to the throne? The niece or the granddaughter? Whom do you select?' I posed a question to her, but she couldn't come to a conclusion. The granddaughter? Or the niece? I made the question candid. Yet she thought for a long time.

"'It's the power conflict.' Uma remained silent; perhaps no one could answer it. Legally it was the grand daughter's right. But Vasundhara had answered it by her tricks to waive the other. 'How could she be so cruel?' said Uma.

"'Power makes man a bully,' I said dispassionately. 'Power makes one corrupt and compassionless.'

"'Women are their victims often,' she said in a soliloquy.

"'We are the worst affected.' I supported her views. 'We were both ill-treated by our kinsmen, not by enemies. But the enemies within are most dangerous.'

The sun was up in the sky. The call of hunger had awakened us too. The children had occupied their places with their bronze plates, making much fuss and eagerly waiting for their turn. The din was terrific, and we couldn't hear each other until the food was served. It marked a difference to put them in the world of segregation. The residents ate and drank as they wished. It fell as a credit upon the Mannanar that no discrimination was allowed in the Aramana. The residents were well-bred and secure. The Makkachiyars had their grooms from the Thiyya youths. Their eldest son could become the Mannanar. The nights in the Aramana were so colourful and rhythmic, with many phases of love blooming in bridal chambers. There seemed to exist a healthy competition among the Makkachiyars as to the reception of their men, and the performance, for each one tried their best to bring out the maximum. The quick breathing and hissing resembled that of cupid's revelry chamber. The fragrance of flowers roused emotions and love play. The Aramana as a whole might have become excited along with its residents in the late hours of the night, and likely to be extended to the wee hours of the day. Even then, the lovers felt that they had shortened nights.

"The wild meat and arrack from the bootleggers added virility to men while their partners enjoyed it very much. Being a lecher himself, the Mannanar would often go in for innocent teen age girls, which caused uproar in the village. This forced the parents to take extra care of their virgin daughters, and they weren't allowed to travel or loiter, and were instructed to stay at home. Girls would shudder to hear his name, avoided visits, and always kept themselves at the rear of the house.

"The word Mannanar was widely used by older people to frighten the naughty children. Though he ruled well and maintained law and order in his jurisdiction, the bad reputation sowed hatred in the minds of his subjects, but never did they dare to confront the master of martial arts. The sudras bore the hatred in them, longed for his elimination and waited, sharpening their hatred. The upper caste people felt ashamed of being governed by a low-bred man and also thirsted for his blood. But the approval of the royal family as the Mannanar helped him to remain in power. During one of his exploratory rides, he spotted a young, lean, charming girl who boiled his passion. Her complexion was golden. Her hair was thick and curly black with beautiful ringlets. She had large black naughty eyes, red lips and a beautiful nose like the parrot's beak. She was sweet and elegant. The very sight fancied his imagination and instigated his lust. Having been blinded by his extreme passion, like an eagle landing upon its prey, he flew down and returned to his cart with the girl who was shocked and dumb with fear. The cart swiftly darted towards the Aramana with its master fisting the girl like an eagle to its prey. The girl was so frightened that she couldn't even scream.

"The people were infuriated to hear the news. The fact that the girl belonged to Sudra's community added fuel to the fire. Congregating in large numbers, they protested, but none dared to face the fury of the Mannanar. In the Aramana, too, the Makkachiyars murmured in protest. Somebody even suggested chopping off his hood and not allowing the little stump to remain, using a sickle to slice it off. Only then would he learn a lesson, each of the Makkachiyar had enjoyed his talents in the art of his love play. The protest against the abduction had been on the rise, but slowly it subsided like the screaming over the loss of the beloved.

"The girl was locked in a small room at the end of the vestibule, facilitated with all provisions, well-furnished and decorated. But she remained defiant and revengeful and completely lost hope. The Mannanar was full of hope and waited impatiently for the good turn. But it seemed she would never recover. Day by day her condition grew worse. She had refused to eat food, drank only a little water, and always seemed sad and thoughtful. With the help of his faithful Makkachiyars, he made several unsuccessful brutal attempts to feed her, all in vain. The frustrated Mannanar committed many foolish deeds but couldn't conquer her mind. Hearing her screaming, I rushed to her room only to see four women forcefully trying to feed her. They pushed rice into her gullet and poured water into her mouth to wash it down.

"'Stop it!' I roared. They shuddered and gazed at me in wonder. 'What have you been doing to her?' I shouted. I was trembling with anger. All of them remained silent. 'If anything happens to her, you will have to answer for it,' I warned them.

"The women left the room one after the other, muttering, 'Who's this, superior to the Mannanar?' one of them said.

"'A saviour has come to her rescue,' another said while making a face at me.

"I sat beside the girl, cleaned her face and wiped away her tears. It seemed that she was sleeping unconsciously. So many days of fasting had left her exhausted, and only slender breathing existed in her. I feared something would happen. I sprinkled water on her face and fanned her. To my surprise, she opened her eyes slowly.

"Her half-opened eyes feebly turned to me, asking, 'What have I done to deserve this?'

"But words wouldn't come out of her throat. They were obstructed. Tears rolled down her cheeks, and she screamed.

"'You haven't lost anything,' I tried to console her.

"'Haven't I?' she responded. Then she said, 'I lost everything except me,' she said, sobbing. I could understand her strength of character, which I valued very much.

So I said, 'Being abducted to the Kotta never meant that you lost everything.' I tried to make her cope with the realities.

"'Haven't I lost my home? My parents and my friends? They are all alien to me. For them, I'm a lost one.'

"'Don't be so frustrated, Parvathy,' I said, caressing her cheeks and wiping her tears.

"'I wish I were dead,' she lamented.

"Softly patting her shoulder, I tried to pacify her sobbing heart, all in vain. Then I challenged her. 'I bet you don't know how I got here.'

"At once, it began to work. She stopped sobbing abruptly and agreed with me, nodding her head.

"'And you estimate me as a Makkachiyar?' I hinted.

"'Aren't you a Makkachiyar?' was her sudden response. She might have thought that all the ladies in the Kotta were

Makkachiyars, and I was one. A ray of hope splashed through her face. She raised her eyes and looked at me curiously, which seemed to ask, 'Then who are you?'

"I didn't want to repeat my story to everyone. So I said, 'I was a victim of a conspiracy.'

"She listened to me earnestly. Something went into her head. 'A victim?'

"'Yeah! Of course, a victim in the true sense.' I totally agreed with her.

"'But you face the things as a warrior,' she complimented, and I smiled at her.

"'It is something like, your mind, asserting the truth,' I said.

"The Kotta slowly awakened from the drowsiness of a mid-summer afternoon. Makkachiyars were preparing for their bath in the river. Some were smearing oil all over their bodies. Some took their clothes to be washed. Young women smeared green gram paste on their faces and were making '*Thali*[39]' to wash their hair. Swimming and frolicking in the luminescent water, which was slightly reddish gold and rippling, excited the slushy greenish banks on either side. The trees rained flowers on them. They went on until the red blaze of the sun began to vanish slowly.

"Mannanar was out in the *kalari,* inspecting the men in practice and giving instructions to the *Gurukkal*, for making the *kalaries* strong and dynamic. He feared a rebellion within. He knew the vindictiveness of the Sudras towards him was unabating like that of the rutting tusker.

The abduction of the girl, Parvathy, had widely aroused contempt and displeasure. It had fuelled the grudge and hatred he had already been facing from the upper castes. During the winter,

---

[39] A herbal paste to be made by women to clean their hair.

even the trees shrink. Who else wishes to do without a partner? It was the time for revelry in the Aramana. Makkachiyars would prepare something special for the occasion, to rouse their emotions. The hooch and wild meat added vigour.

"The winter passed by, and summer was on the way. It was expected that every resident should attend with their partners in the Cupid Pooja to be held in the month of Meenam at the Aramana. Parvathi and me were in a fix. We didn't have partners. Accepting one from the thiyya community and becoming a Makkachiyar would be easy, but as we didn't want to become Makkachiyars, we thought avoidance would be better.

"'Parvathi, you must have your meal?' I said.

"But at the same time, I doubted whether my tone was that of an authoritarian. Her pale face became paler, and then she said, 'I won't eat a morsel until I am let out.' She was very bold, though weak in physique.

"'But how long can you hold on?' I gazed at her and said.

"'Until my last breath.'

"She was determined. But I was helpless. I had never seen such a bold girl in my life, and I was afraid that the girl might lose her life. It began to make my heart ache. I felt that I must get involved. I must talk to the Mannanar to let her go. He had been out during the day and would reach the Kotta very late. I was perplexed so much that my heart ached. I kept waiting eagerly for him. When the Mannanar finally arrived, he was intoxicated and his feet unsteady. I grew even more perplexed. I couldn't resist my inner voice. Daringly I approached him.

"He seductively said, 'Oh! You have come. I know you will come.'

"Then he tried to get up from his seat. Daringly I faced him. I thought I could meet the situation.

"'The abducted girl is dying,' I said to him.

"'Dying?' he said, surprised.

"'Yeah! Dying through fasting?' I replied.

"'Didn't she eat anything?' he anxiously asked.

"'Not even a morsel yet,' I said. 'It is like walking on a tightrope. She may fall at any time.' As soon as I said it, I turned and quickly walked away to my room.

"Before bolting the door, I went to her and made her drink some water and told her that I had talked to him. I couldn't sleep that night. When I got up the next morning, a little late, I didn't find Parvathi where she had been. My heartbeat rose. I was eager to know what had happened to her. Dead or alive, nobody seemed to know. Yet I dared not go to him again. An unknown fear began to engulf me gradually; I even looked at the shadows suspiciously. The incident pushed the Kotta into a world of chaos, and rumours were rife.

People feared the Kotta. They wouldn't go into or near to it. The sun was going to set. The shadows became longer, and the water in the river turned dark. The weather was hot, and women and children spent most of their day in the river. Women washed their clothes and spread them on the shores to dry. They then rested in the cool shade. Children played in the water, splashing and sprinkling. Some were engaged in fishing using the fleshy leaf stalk.

Never had it been so isolated from the people. The Mannanar never thought he was at fault, but went to the astrologer for guidance. Spreading the cowrie and setting them in trio on the twelve signs of the Zodiac, the Astrologer told him that the time was not good for him. Saturn was in the ascendance; it would constantly harass him, and there would be calamities and misfortunes. There would be an attack on the Kotta. The misfortune had begun as a result of the entrance of a woman from the west into the Aramana, and she should be expelled. A Sathru Samhara *Pooja*[40] should be conducted in the Kotta for the destruction of his enemies.

"As days passed Mannanar was in a fix. A large quantity of water had flowed down the river. His grave concern was finding out who the lady from the west was. He began to analyse the data regarding the whereabouts of the lady residents. For the whole day and night, he thought, analysed and tried to correlate the problems with them. At last, he came to a conclusion. It was none other than me who brought the misfortunes to him, but he didn't spell it out to anyone. Even the head Makkachiyar remained aloof from the conviction, and he looked for a chance for my expulsion. Moreover, I wouldn't surrender to him. I was always surrounded by a group of women, and that also irked him. The dos and don'ts also might have infuriated him. He thought I would be an extra burden to the Kotta if not expelled.

The opportunity for this disguised itself as a dreadful disease in the village. Beating drums announcements were made by authorities as precaution. People were advised to clean their homes and land by burning the waste home materials as a step against infection. They were advised to use neem leaves and neem oil in their food.

"Yet '*Kurumba Devi*' spread the disease. Many thought of it as the Devi's anger, but a few believed it was her blessings. Too many died. Those who were severely affected were abandoned in huts away from the village, and they became easy prey and decayed there for torment by tiny animals or decayed until they died. A pall of gloom covered in black pervaded everywhere. People were confined to Pooja in an effort to stop the spread of

---

[40] Pooja for the destruction of the enemies.

the disease. There was much sadness over the loss of near and dear ones. For several, their hopes and dreams were burnt in the funeral pyre along with the diseased. But the '*Kurumba Bagavathi*' preferred the dead to be buried in '*Bhandarams*'. Such stone vault graves became a common feature of the village. People ignited oil lamps at the feet of the *Bhandarams* at dusk.

"All of a sudden, I felt seriously ill. I thought my head would burst because of severe pain, and I felt severely chilled. Entering my room, I lay in my bed with covers on me. Soon after, I slipped into a world of oblivion. How long I slept, I didn't know. When I woke up in the middle of the night, I was sweating heavily and felt thirsty and badly in need of water. I couldn't find anyone to bring me water to quench my thirst. I tried to get up but fainted. I couldn't stand up for long. I fell on my cot and struggled to get back memories.

"The beetles woke me, and it was completely dark. I couldn't see anything. I was aching all over my body. When I passed my fingers over my skin, I felt that there were furuncles all over, without even an inch of intervening space. A cool wind blew in. I couldn't make out where I was. My eyelids remained closed as I couldn't open them; there were furuncles on them too. Suddenly I heard a growling in the distance, and I shuddered. I didn't know if it was day or night. I couldn't open my eyes because the rheum in my eyes had stuck my eyelids together. Slowly, with the tip of my fingers, I tried to remove the rheum, which I eventually managed. I was frightened. I was in the middle of the forest, in a hut on stakes halfway up a tree. The sun was slowly emerging out from behind the hillock. It was all reddish gold, and the hillock seemed to erupt up to the sky like a large black cloud surrounded by a halo of golden sunbeams.

"Soon it occurred to my timid mind that I had been

mercilessly dumped in the woods. Helplessly I lay perhaps with a diminishing consciousness, exhausted with hunger and thirst. No sound of human was heard anywhere near, only the cooing of the birds and the trickling sounds of the rivulet. I couldn't remember anything." Rajalakshmi narrated her story, and the girls were amazed.

Chapter 5

All soaked in the mist, the hillock remained sleepy during the winter. People got up late and went to bed early. They kept a fireplace burning in their homes and sat around it chatting, drinking hootch and eating roasted pork and wild roots, smearing salt and turmeric on large pieces of pigmeat and skewering it on a long spit; they waited impatiently. Enjoying the charring of the pig meat, sometimes sneezing because of the penetrating smell of burnt chilly, Peasants engaged in gossip during the evenings. Winter had compelled them to remain at home.

Kodanddi helped his mother to chop firewood, fetch water from the rivulet or clean home on alternate days. He made the cattle bathe. Kasthuri also helped them. Vellachi wouldn't let her do the risky manual labours. She would often say, "Oh! Princess, let it be there."

But Kasthuri helped them, saying, "I am also eating."

"The sun will wilt your body," Kodanddi said to her while he took the Iron bar. She smiled.

"Where to?" she said.

"For digging roots." He took the basket and chopper in his left hand, placed the iron bar on his right shoulder, and began walking.

"May I come with you?" Kasthuri beseeched him. He looked back and said, "The thorns will hurt your feet."

"I shall take care," she asserted.

"It's so deep. Going down is riskier," he warned her.

"Yeah, I can manage," she said.

He cut a six feet tall staff and gave it to her to help her while walking downward.

They went down together like two adjacent rivulets joining and rushing down to the destination. He stopped abruptly when he found an ideal place abundant in wild roots. Spotting a wild root stump, he set the basket and the chopper aside and began to dig. It was so big and had so many branch roots it took much time and energy to dig out the roots, and even under the cool shade, Kodanddi sweated and was smeared with mud all over. When finished, the basket became full of fleshy, juicy roots oozing blood-like fluid.

She sat on a rock all the time until it was finished.

"It's of a superior kind," he said. "Nutritious and tasty," he added.

She didn't know anything about wild roots. So she was silent. After a while, she said, "We have a lot of yam and colocasia. So why do you toil so much?"

"It's medicinal and good for health," he said.

Kodanddi carried the loaded basket to the stream to wash out the soil sticking to the roots. Together they washed them thoroughly and kept them in the basket to drain. Then he plunged into the icy cold water which came above his waist.

"Kasthuri," Kodanddi called her at the top of his voice. It echoed on the nearby hills.

He glanced at her, and she realised he was inviting her in. She felt embarrased.

"Kodanddi," she responded, and her voice also echoed on the hills. Soon the two sounds reverberated simultaneously. Stripping to her underwear, she too plunged into the water and dove in. They spent a lot of time frolicking and splashing in the water.

When they embraced, they felt the heat of their passion for

each other. She kissed him on his forehead. The chilliness of the water couldn't alleviate the heat. The fragrance of the wild flowers induced them. The mist that came from somewhere else, they didn't know where for certain, screened the rivulet as if it were a bridal chamber, decorated with the bunches of wild flowers carrying fragrance and honeydews. A gentle breeze swept over them, bringing floral rain. Kodanddi kissed her on her cheek, neck and everywhere he could. They writhed and wriggled.

Before the sun went down, they climbed up the hillock carrying the basket full of roots, which would normally bring a contented smile to Vellachi's wrinkled face, but this time it was cloudy black; it seemed like a look of fury.

Kodanddi placed the basket full of roots in front of her and said, "Amma, look at this."

"Kolu kondu thudakku nalu pedachal nee padikkum," (You will learn only when you get four cuts on your thigh with a cane.) she burst out.

"Why Amma?" he said. It was so polite as to melt even a stone heart.

"Thamburatty Kuttyem kootty monthikku kattilu nadakkuka," (You wander in the woods with Thamburatty Kutty at night.) she again burst out with anger and concern.

"Oh! That is the matter. We have been looking for roots in the woods. After digging, we took a bath in the rivulet too," he explained.

"Kattu kizhengu! Mannankatta." (Wild root, Clod.) Kodanddi couldn't pacify the heat of her anger.

Kasthuri, still bearing the sweet languors of the revelry, stepped forward and said, "We were nearby, Amma. We didn't go too far."

The cloudy black face began to shine as if the sky shone after the boisterous rainfall during the *Thulavarsham* (Northeast monsoon).

"*Nariyum, Puliyum, pambumundu kattil*[41]," Vellachi told her. Then she prayed. "*Mala Daivangale, Nagakanni Katholane.*"[42]

Kodanddi felt sleepy. He yawned, then he said, "Oh! I feel sleepy. Let's have our supper."

Kasthuri, too, felt tired and wanted to go to bed but went into the kitchen to help Vellachi. But Vellachi, too timid to assign her any work in the kitchen, said, "Oh! My little princess, go and have a nap. When it is ready, I will call you."

Vellachi was in a jubilant mood, for Kodanddi had exempted himself from several proposals, but now he has hit the bull's eye. She thought that the good deeds of his past life might have honoured him by giving the princess as his bride. Although she had a thousand tongues to talk about Kasthuri, whom he met wherever it might be; she smelt a rat, a confusion remained her mind.

They heard her call while they were sinking into the depths of sleep. Yet they got up and tasted the delicious dinner prepared with motherly love and affection. The tiredness added to sleep made them silent even while they ate the nourishing roasted roots dipped in condiment. As soon as they finished their meals, they went to bed, leaving Vellachi alone with the starry night.

Suddenly Velachi heard the crushing of the bamboo groves. She shuddered. She went out and listened, sensing from the pungent odour of the dung the presence of a herd of elephants, a rare threat on the steep hillock. Anticipating the danger, she

---

[41] There are tigers, leopards and snakes in the woods.
[42] The Mountain gods, Nagakanni, protect us.

decided to wake her son up. But it was unlikely after the day's hard work because he would usually sink into a sound sleep from which no one could wake him up.

Vellachi, as usual, resorted to calling up the Goddesses of the mountain to save them. She feared that after crushing the bamboo groves, the elephants might turn towards the human habitats, and their huts, crops and belongings would be ruined by a stampede.

The danger was at their doorstep, but Kodanddi wouldn't get up. She couldn't shout loudly for fear that the shouts might provoke the herd. Then she went out in the dark as she had a sense of the herd, although she couldn't see them.

Though she couldn't see anything specific, she understood they were at the groves munching bamboo like sugarcane. Again she went in to wake her son but kept back seeing the door bolted from inside. She knocked on the door gently, but this yielded no result.

Again she went out in the dark, only to hear the crushing of the bamboo, and felt the pungent smell of the dung penetrating her nostrils but consoled herself that the herd was still in the bamboo groves.

Kodanddi had piled up hundreds of rocks on the hillock in such a way that their weight propped up one key rock, which was supported by a lever. It was tied to a tree by a strong rope. If the lever was pulled out using the rope, the key rock would be turned down, and all the hundreds of rocks would rush down, gathering momentum and making the elephants take to their heels and scatter.

Taking it for granted as a natural calamity, the elephants wouldn't return for retaliation and would likely stay away owing to fear. The danger had reached their doorstep, and Vellachi felt hopelessly disappointed. Still, she made efforts to wake her son-

and daughter-in-law. Hopefully, she could somehow awaken her royal daughter-in-law, Kasthuri, who could wake up her husband from sleep.

Kodanddi groaned and said angrily, "Why do you bang so hard?"

"It's all because of the wild elephant, dear."

Kasthuri opened the door, and Vellachi entered, panting as though she had been running all the time, and her breasts bobbed up and down vigorously. The fear and anxiety made her weep.

"Mom, Don't weep like this," he consoled her. "If they come closer, I'll let loose the rocks."

"They are still at the groves, I think," said Kasthuri. "The herd will turn away after finishing the groves," she opined.

"But the tusker may be dangerous. We should be cautious," he warned.

In the mist, it was difficult to see them, especially the tusker, who may stand still along the wayside, easily making humans accessible. The stamping of the footsteps and the sounds of the plucking and munching of bamboo like the sugar cane were heard a long way off. The steaming dung spread its unbearable pungent smell. The wind carried it everywhere, cautioning the people.

When the first rays of the sun broke out from the eastern horizon, the people turned up in large numbers to assess the extent of the destruction.

"Fortunately, they didn't enter the human habitat," One elder man sighed.

"But we must be careful," opined another.

"Why can't we dig a moat on the wood's side?" proposed Kodanddi.

"It's a good idea," several supported the idea.

"We must think it over," Kothumban, who had once been

Kodanddi's right hand, said.

"If all of us come together, it can be worked out successfully."

The anxiety over their safety compelled them to come together and dig a ditch on the woods side of their village.

They dispersed, agreeing to meet the next day, anxiety and fear still prevailing on them.

Kasthuri was still in her bed. The fatigue and langour still clung to her. Their sleep had been disrupted the previous night. The elephants had taken away their peace of mind along with their sleep.

Fearing the tusker, they couldn't go down into the woods. Hunting of the wild boar and digging of roots had come to a halt, and many of the folks had to tighten their loincloths.

Famine would lead to infectious diseases and deaths. Kodanddi feared.

Hunting, covering a large area of the woods, was being planned by the locals of that area. It would be a double boon to the simple-minded peasants as it would not only enable them to gather sumptuous edible meat, but also drive away the wild beasts as well, settling their fears.

They lined up as many men as they could with country guns, several with bows and arrows and many with spears and poles. The whole village was involved, and it looked like Buppidal on the occasion of *Kathivannur Veeran* Theyyam Kettu[43].

Accordingly, an area that used to be an animal habitat was marked on the festival of a prominent Theyyam, Kathivannur veeran, this Theyyam represents a great warrior, his prowess and is surrounded by gunmen and archers'. Men with spears and

---

[43] The festival of prominent Theyyam Kathivannur veeran, a great warrior.

poles would enter the woods with their hounds. For hours the woods reverberated with the barking of the dogs and shouting of men.

The whole of the woods trembled so horribly that even the bravest beast would take to its heels. The men, hiding with their guns or bows, would aim at them. Several rounds of firing, howling and shouts could be heard.

It was a big catch. Their enthusiasm was so high and remarkable. The speed of the intrusion didn't affect the accuracy of their aim.

Wild boars and elks were in their catch. Kodanddi could aim at an animal and shoot at the right front shoulder bone even when it was speeding so that the animal couldn't even move one step ahead. It would fall down on the spot. Another point of his aim was behind the ear of the animal, which would make it spin and fall at an uncontrollable speed.

As an astute shooter, his name was known among the country folks and he was admired greatly.

His fancy had risen up to hunting a tiger and he was uncompromising – both the tool and its practice. But no chances came his way.

Making a lot of noise, the jubilant folk returned, carrying the catch tied to thick poles by two or three men. Several such loads were brought to the open space, where they assembled and shared the meat.

Being a good shooter, Kodanddi got several heads and back thighs. But accepted a few as per need, the rest being shared off.

Yet many greedy ones wanted more, shamelessly asking for more and accumulated meat sufficient for many days. They could dry the meat in the bright sun and preserve it for the days to come. They all finally had a healthy meal after several months.

Kodanddi separated the tongues of the wild boars from their heads and kept them for drying over the fireplace, dangled like a garland of tongues. The dried tongue could be used as a powerful drug for snake bites. It made him recollect the memories of his father, an eminent snakebite physician, snake bite being a common event then.

The meat of the wild boar was, perhaps, the most delicious of all, not for all but surely for some; Kodanddi being one among them. Charring and peeling was a difficult task as its skin was one to one-and-a-half inches thick, with the hairs being so thick and black causing disgust. He made it neat by scraping and washing it thoroughly. Then he cut it into small pieces, washed it again and checked it, making it devoid of impurities.

Kodanddi then called out to his mother, "Mom, take some for the dish and keep the rest for drying."

Vellachi was astonished to see such a large quantity of meat and took some to her satisfaction. The rest she put in a rattan basket to drain away the water content in it. The bloody water oozed out of the gaps of the basket and flowed down to a small thin rivulet that resembled the tears that trickled down when they were shot dead. Kodanddi felt pity for them.

Kasthuri stood nearby, watching how the dishes were made.

Vellachi mixed the meat with salt, Turmeric and chilly powder, smeared it appropriately, kept it for some time and waited for the ingredients to soak in.

In the meantime, she took the rest of the meat kept for draining in the rattan basket, mixed it with salt and Turmeric powder, spread it in the hanging rattan just above the fireplace, put some thick firewood in the hearth and ignited it. The smoke and heat would dry the meat within a few days.

What astonished Kasthuri, though, was that Vellachi did

many things simultaneously; nothing seemed to lose her care and attention. Putting the spicy meat in the frying pan, she blew the air to get the firewood to burn steadily. Then she stirred the meat with a small flat wooden ladle. She went on stirring the meat until it turned coppery brown and to smelt inviting which made them salivate.

Suddenly they spotted Kodanddi vomiting. Rushing to him, they enquired, "What? Why are you vomiting?" Vellachi caressed his back and examined his eyes and tongue. At once she went in and brought a pinch of pepper powder.

"What's that?" he said

"Pepper," she answered and said, "Open your mouth."

When he opened his mouth, she put the pepper powder in and asked him to munch.

Having not felt its bitter taste, he said, "No, Mom, it's not pepper but sawdust."

Thunder-stricken Vellachi was shocked and snarled at him but was convinced at once of snake bite.

Vellachi and Kasthuri examined his body all over and detected a small swelling on his left calf and two adjacent needle like stings, which summoned immediate treatment.

He was so vigorous and enthusiastic during the course of hunting and might not have noticed it, Vellachi thought, "Oh! My Naga Kanni!" she lamented.

"You didn't protect him. Every day at dawn and dusk, I pray to you, but you didn't lend your ears to my prayer." Lamenting, she beat her chest hard several times.

Kasthuri, so perplexed, didn't know what to do but tried to prevent her from beating on her breast.

Extremely frightened and nervous, Vellachi rushed to

Kothumban's hut, panting and sweating. Words wouldn't come out of her throat. But somehow she conveyed what had happened, and within the wink of an eye, many men turned up with a large wooden armchair to carry their much-adored leader to the *Vishahari* miles away.

The wild boar's tongue, which had been dried, was ground and made into a paste; a part of it was smeared in the bitten area and the rest given to drink.

"Let's go, Kodanddi," Kothumban said when everything was ready.

But Kodanddi said tiredly, "I don't have any problem just a little tired." There was something that made him very fatigued.

"You vomited, didn't you?" said Kothumban.

"Everyone vomits," a smiling Kodanddi said slowly, which made others laugh.

"This is not the time for a joke," Kothumban became serious.

"Haven't you noticed the stings on his calf?" he raised his voice and looked at the others.

"Again, why is this swelling?"

They looked at each other. No one spoke. Then Vellachi came forward and said, "Take him to the *Vishahari* soon, children."

Kasthuri sobbed in anguish. But she restrained herself so as not to break down.

Finally, Kodanddi agreed. Bearing him in the armchair, they set off to the *Vishahari,* a tedious task with steep ups and downs. But the youths who loved him much were ready to cast off even their hearts for him.

They wished they would have moved faster than the gales, which always pooh-poohed the mountain with the monstrous chilly air or the tigers galloping after their prey. Before dark, they reached the hut that stood in the middle of the woods, where vines spread over the trees and gave a cool shade to the courtyard. Four or five children with tangled hair and running mucus played in the courtyard, of which three were girls.

The courtyard had been swept clean all around the hut. Several stone idols of Nagaraja and Nagakanny were placed under a tree with two stone lamps in front of them with half-burnt wicks.

The bearers entered the courtyard. Uppichi Narayani, the *Vishahari* was in the kitchen. The children ran inside to inform her.

Hearing the human voices, a rare occasion in the woods, Uppichi came out and went straight to the man lying on the cow dung-smeared verandah. Examining him thoroughly, she spotted the two stings oozing blood slightly.

Chewing pan as a habit, her lips were red, and the two sharp serpentine eyes glittered between the plum blackberry cheeks and curly black hair.

"When did it happen?" she said, scanning them with her penetrating looks.

"This morning, while he was hunting in the woods," Kothumban answered, not looking at her. In fact, he dared not face her piercing eyes.

"By the grace of God, you are here!" she exclaimed. Kodanddi groaned as if he was half conscious.

"Otherwise, you won't be here," she said to the impatient bearers. The reptile was so venomous it could have finished even the elephants in no time, they were told. During the course of hunting at great speed, perhaps Kodanddi mightn't have noticed, or the reptile hadn't got enough time to inject its venom fully into his body. Only a very negligible portion of the venom had entered.

The Vishahari began to work. From the woods, she brought some medicinal leaves, ground them into a paste and placed it thickly in the middle of his head and made him place his bitten calf in a wooden bucket half filled with icy cold crystal clear water.

They watched the water in the wooden bucket and, holding their breath, impatiently waited for the result. They could see a thin flow of blood from the sting contaminated with venom, not red but bluish-red in colour, slowly diffused into the water and turned it bluish red.

Uppichi had disappeared into the woods to pluck herbal leaves again. She turned up after an hour or so, squeezing the leaves in between her palms and rolling it into a ball. She put it into her own mouth and began to chew for some time. Then she wiped the stings on the calf with a piece of cloth, and putting her lips on the stung area tightly, she sucked the contaminated blood into her mouth and spat it out. She repeated the process several times and looked like a fairy woman sucking blood from the charmed. Her lips were blood smeared, hair widely apart, and clothes worn out. But she was confident of the cure.

Washing out the wound incessantly in a flow of water and soothing with medicinal herbs, Uppichi tried her best, but Kodanddi felt as if he had been hit heavily on his head. She said he will be fine in a week's time. The treatment should be continued, putting them in a fix, she added, "Venom has entered his brain slightly." She looked at him. Spitting the chewed betel and areca nut off her mouth, she continued, "That's why the giddiness." She observed.

"Won't it subside?" asked Kothumban eagerly.

"Oh! Sure, but takes time," Uppichi told them. Then she

gave medicines to drink three times a day for three days and herbal paste to smear on the sting.

Uppichi directed them, "Come on the fourth day with chicks and luck. He'll be all right then." Carrying Kodanddi on the armchair and saying "goodbye" to the children and Uppichi, the bearers climbed down the hillock. They felt relieved and were happy to hear he will be okay, but were ready to throw away their lives at his feet if necessary.

Vellachi and Kasthuri waited anxiously for them without food and drink, praying in tears and offerings to the gods they knew.

Climbing down the hillock was tougher than the upward task. The slightest slide might endanger one's life, making him fall into the deep pitch, never to be seen again.

Somehow they came down carrying Kodanddi. The medicines had begun their work and the giddiness slightly receded.

On reaching home, Vellachi wouldn't allow them to take leave without having their stomachs filled.

Drinking two or three bowls of porridge made of millet, Kodanddi took rest. On closing his eyes, all the scenes of hunting flashed through his mind. But nowhere could he trace even a doubt of snake bite. Kodanddi began to talk, and that relieved them much.

Vellachi made him drink the medicines as per the instructions of the Vishahari. Perhaps she was even stricter than her. Kasthuri attended to him with sincere love though she didn't know anything of the sort.

Vellachi was active, had an intuition, and would become more active in such critical situations as if she knew the need of the hour.

For three days, they spent their entire time looking after him with timely medicines and rest. The giddiness slowly subsided, and his senses returned. But his body fatigue didn't to leave him completely, and they thought it might be because he was eating less.

Kothumban and other youngsters would come occasionally enquiring about the improvement of his condition. Seeing the improvement, they all became happy. They wanted their Kodanddi to be smarter. And on the fourth day, when they came to carry him up to go to the Vishahari Narayani, Kodanddi was reluctant. He was ready to walk all the way.

The Seven-men party set off with Kodanddi and several cocks and hens. There were bottles of hootch too. They carried the sacks of rice in line. The journey looked like a pilgrimage atop the mountain.

Uppichi Narayani was so pleased to see Kodanddi was better. She examined his eyes and tongue. Her pleasure doubled when she found that they had brought huge gifts for her.

Children flocked around the chicks. Uppichi beseeched the party to sit on the raised platform and gave them ginger coffee to drink.

She gave Kodanddi medicines along with instructions, perhaps more than the previous time. They talked for some time. Before taking leave, Kodanddi gave her a gold coin as a present. Her face beamed.

On their return, they were jubilant. Cracking jokes, the noisy seven climbed down the hill. On the way, Kodanddi thought that his experience was a strange one, never heard of before, a snake bite without a snake or the snake being invisible. Perhaps such an experience might have been registered in his horoscope. The mountain gods might have saved him from the fatal fate; they couldn't be waivered over without its trace or mark.

That year they had very good rain in the summer, making the farmers commence their work earlier. The peasants were busy on the hill tract. Men and women were engaged in cleaning the woods, burning the waste to ashes and again cleaning, uprooting the stumps and piling them up with the unburnt remnants and burning again. They tried to make the soil fertile and delicate.

Vellachi and Kasthuri joined Kodanddi in the work, and there were many men and women covering their heads with turbans. Bending their backs, they were busily engaged with the choppers and sickles. In the meantime, they quenched their thirst by drinking gruel from their pot gourd bottle.

The rendering of the folk song, which described the peasants as warriors of Siva, resembled battle songs, which pleased Kasthuri.

"The double heat is not suited to you," said Vellachi to Kasthuri.

"Double?" she queried.

"Yes, the heat of the midday sun and that of the fire," Vellachi explained.

"It's just fun, Mom," Kasthuri said lovingly.

"But the sun in the month of *Menam* would burn you," Vellachi warned her.

"It doesn't matter, Mom. Now I'm one among you," she said.

It seemed that she had forgotten all about her past and the good old lady wanted to retain it since she was so proud of it.

They were making the hill tract land ready for sowing the paddy. The stumps and roots, along with the parts of the unburned wood, had been piled up for burning again. The fire would destroy all the germs, and the ashes would make the land fertile.

Moreover, the weeds would be less if burnt properly.

The heat of the sun and the fire made them to looking like black apes. But if they rested in the month of Menam and Medam, they would have to take rest for the whole year with nothing to eat. The seeds of the grains, pulses and vegetables would be sowed in the hill tract field in the season and would be reaped at the rate of hundred, enough to feed them for a whole year.

At other times some would be engaged in hunting, a few in the extraction of honey or forest goods and a very few in the distilling of hootch. If they harvested abundantly, they would rejoice the whole year; otherwise, they would be compelled to lead a hand-to-mouth life.

"When will the sowing be done?" Kasthuri asked.

"*Ente Tampuratty Kutty, Medathil withu kilachal chingathil mooram*[44]," Vellachi said. Her words sprouted young wings to their expectations.

Kothumban wiped his sweat with a piece of cloth, which he had been using as a turban. "The soil is very fertile," he said. "It can breed at the rate of a hundred," he added.

"*Mannum Pennum nannakkiyal nannakum,*"[45] Vellachi prophesied.

Vellachi glanced at Kasthuri, and she didn't know what could be said about her. The evening sun had reddened her body, making it shine. Her curly hair fluttered in the breeze. When their shadows became longer and longer, they returned to their homes with their utensils, only to return the next day.

Everything went well on the hillock since the weather was

---

[44] My little princess, if you sow in the month of Medam, we can reap the harvest in the month of chingam.
[45] Soil and women improve gloriously if treated better.

fine. One could see people digging, chopping and burning everywhere.

Kasthuri could understand the sweat and panting of the peasant men in their striving for a living, the true nature of the life of country folk.

They had a dip in the rivulet before they reached home. The cool, crystal clear water washed away the sweat and soil smeared on them. But their simple life was clearer than the water in the rivulet that flowed down the mountain to its sole destination. The cool fresh water refreshed them.

The breeze pacified the hot flat rock not far away from their home. Yet it was warm. Kodanddi and Kasthuri were leaning on it. She embraced him.

"Does my sweat stink?" he said.

"No, not a little, but smells manly," she said as if she liked it.

"Feel pain?" he asked.

"You are as soft as flower petals of screwpine," Kodanddi said, caressing her slowly with his calloused palm.

"Not at all," she said. Actually, she was enjoying the roughness of his hardened palm.

Their love play continued for a long time until they heard Vellachi calling them for supper.

Chapter 6

An Alata tree bearing a lot of reddish brown flowers in bunches but surely not at all shady as a persimmon stood high up among other trees. It bore no fragrance but was blessed with honey and pollen. On the slanting branches, there lay several large Pandanus leaf mats like honeycombs dangling, which summoned the attraction and curiosity of the peasants. The humming sound of the bees reverberated around while the peasants longingly looked at it. The precarious position atop warranted trepidation and forced them to keep away from making an attempt for extraction.

Kodanddi, like many, had an eye upon it, and too many dissuaded him for fear of the consequences that would occur. But he earnestly kept his wish unabated and looked for an appropriate time to carry out his difficult task. He never shared his plan with his mother or Kasthuri, for he knew their love and affection would throw up hurdles. It had to be extracted before the beginning of the rain, he thought; otherwise, the honey would be lost.

Kodanddi began to make urgent arrangements secretly and astutely made a long rope of wild creepers to reach from top to bottom of the Alata. It resembled an elephant rope, and he made sharp metal strips to pierce the trunk of the Alata and cut large bamboo drums for collecting the honey. He disclosed his denouement to no one other than Kothumban.

He smeared the herbal paste all over its body to keep the bees away. That was precaution to be safe from sting. This was prepared, from medicinal leaves from the woods. The work could be done only at night.

He thought of kerosene lanterns that would be helpful to light up the dark night and went ahead with his plan. He had sent word to Kothumban, his sincere aid, to be available that night, but he didn't want to force him.

As it grew dark, Kodanddi, along with Kothumban, reached the spot. Clearing the weeds and the plants under the Alata in the light of the lantern, they brought the necessary things. Instructing Kothumban to climb up a nearby tree with his gun, he said, "Listen for tigers; they may jump out."

"Shall I shoot at it?" Kothumban asked eagerly.

"No, not at first, only when it is necessary."

Bearing the gun, Kothumban climbed atop a tree that stood nearby.

Kodanddi hammered in a nail on the tree and hung the lantern on it. Then he took metal strips and thrashed them to the Alata tree in such a way that each strip could be used as a step to climb up the tree. The striking echoed in the woods. He raised the lantern and hung it higher, carrying the roll of the rope on his shoulder again. He thrashed four or five metal strips so that he could step up.

It went on for a long time until he reached the top. Holding his breath, Kothumban waited.

As Kodanddi went up, he could hear the buzzing of the bees. He tied one end of the rope to the trunk at the top.

Then he climbed down through the metal strip steps holding the rope. Tying the bamboo drums to the rope with strings, he went up and pulled them up. The honey drums were tied to the branches one by one, and they dangled in the air. Then he chewed some herbal leaves and blew the air at the honeycomb. The buzzing bees moved slowly. Sensing the risk, some bees flew around his head but didn't sting. The blowing went on until the bees moved to the far side comfortably. Kodanddi began to pluck off the honeycombs and put them in the bamboo drums. He was amazed to see the abundance of honey. But he never hurt the little ones or the eggs of the bees.

Kothumban heard some movement in the woods and was alert. Informing Kodanddi, he pointed his gun towards the place of movement. Keeping the gun ready, he waited to see what turned up, but in the dim light of the lantern, it was unclear. After some time, a large cat striped in brown and black turned up growling. Turning around and looking up towards the area once or twice, it grunted. Kothumban, holding his breath, held the tree tight. He feared the gun would fall.

Kodanddi looked down. In the dim light of the lantern hung at the lower part of the Alata trunk, he saw the animal looking up.

He could guess that the animal had come for its share. Plucking a large honeycomb abundant with honey and pollen, he climbed a few steps down and put it right into the animal's gaping mouth. Holding the trickling honeycomb, it slowly got lost in the woods, contented and happy. Kodanddi could judge by its expression.

The bamboo drums were dangling full of honey and honeycombs, sweet and fragrant and capable of charming every living being.

The endeavour being over, Kodanddi tied the bamboo honey drums with the rope and descended slowly, one by one. Kothumban received them with utmost care. Bearing the lantern, Kodanddi climbed down slowly, taking off the metal strips that he used as steps for climbing up.

He came down completely exhausted and sweating after

several hours of the tedious task, took rest for a while, and set off for home carrying the honey drums, two each. Kothumban held a lit country torch and Kodanddi moved with lantern in front in the early hours of the day. The night owls had begun their retreat, and the wild cocks howled.

Vellachi was unhappy those days for his over-adventurous actions. Wild meat and wild honey were his weaker points. Kasthuri and Vellachi waited anxiously for them, the former praying to all the mountain gods and the latter walking up and down with worry, even in the early hours of the day. She knew for certain that he has been engaged in a serious task. Otherwise, he wouldn't have stayed away from home.

But what her concern was his adventurous nature, in which he wouldn't mind even risking his own life.

They heard the wailing of the midnight hawk, and Vellachi shuddered. She thought it a bad omen; their anxiety deepened, which made their lamenting more shrill and sharp.

The lantern light from a distance gave life to their expectations. The minutes were endless. They waited in silence.

The duo turned up sighing, all sweaty and carrying the heavy loads of honey brimming to the edges of the bamboo drums, and smiled at them.

Switching to her sweetened tone, Vellachi said, "You have been in the woods?"

"Yeah, Mom," Kodanddi answered.

"But how long? The sun is going up in the sky."

Kasthuri couldn't conceal her anxiety.

"We couldn't finish it up early," Kothumban interrupted.

"What?" Kasthuri said. Her anxiety rose high. "But it's too much," Kasthuri murmured.

"What? The honey? Or the pollen?" Kothumban couldn't

bear the disgusting remarks. He reacted.

For them, it was a great victorious day. Perhaps, nobody other than Kodanddi could have done it so well.

"You needn't go in the rivulet now," Vellachi said. Kodanddi raised his eyes at her. "There is warm water in the cauldron. You can take bath in it," she continued.

Kodanddi and Kothumban took bath in the warm water, which took away their fatigue. The hot rice porridge shed off their tiredness. The cool gentle breeze fanned them.

They placed the honey drums in the interior, making sure ants could not enter them, and placed them in flat vessels with a little water in the bottom.

"You look sleepy," Kasthuri said, seeing Kothumban yawning.

Kodanddi spread a grass mattress on the verandah, and Kasthuri retreated to her bed for a nap.

The morning sun made them jump up out of the mattresses. Kodanddi had never slept after the sunrise till that day. He felt ashamed and hurriedly proceeded to his daily routine.

The processing of honey remained to be completed. Kodanddi cleaned the large jars and wiped them well with a piece of clean cloth to avoid moisture. Then they were placed in the bright sun to dry.

Kothumban was quiescent, still sleeping on the mattress.

"Let him sleep," Kodanddi thought, for it was a boon to sleep; forgetting his worries. Sometimes he would feel envy towards him.

When he went in to fetch a piece of new rough cloth for squeezing the honeycomb. Kasthuri sniffed at him. He glanced at her and said

"Does it stink?"

"No, I am enjoying the fragrance of honey," she came closer to him and smelt him. It seemed to intoxicate her.

Restraining himself, he came out smiling gratefully at her.

Then he took a jar from the sun and, placing it conveniently, took out the bamboo drums filled with honeycombs. Sitting comfortably, he squeezed the combs wrapped in the rough cloth. He never thought of the beautiful precision of the honeycombs but was careful of the eggs and mites present in the comb while squeezing and piled up the wax after squeezing it into a rattan basket. Slowly the honey began to fill the jar. When it was full, he put its lid on and kept it aside. Then he took another one and began to squeeze the honey into it. The whole process was repeated until the last honeycomb was squeezed. Half a dozen jars were full to the brim when completed, and it had taken half of the day. He carried the jars to the inner room and kept them safe. He waited for the forest peddlers to market the honey.

By evening he freed himself. The jars of honey brimming in the inner room would bring a small fortune. But carrying them to the far away market would cost not only a little but the lion's share.

Kothumban also shared his worries. "Let's bottle them first," he suggested.

"New bottles are needed," said Kodanddi.

Then they went out for a walk into the woods to trace the porcupine den. Using the choppers, Kothumban started to cut the thorny bushes and creepers they came upon. But Kodanddi prevented him from doing so.

"Don't, Kothumban," he said.

Kothumban raised his eyebrow at him. He seemed to ask, "Why?"

"It may incite them," Kodanddi said.

"Oh! I never thought of it," Kothumban expressed his ignorance.

Down the hill, they traced a new one, the cleanest and neatest. It seemed that the porcupine has begun the dwelling recently. They identified a rock under which they could hide so they could go poaching at dawn when the animal goes in, or at dusk when it goes out. They were careful not to tamper with the path so that the porcupine wouldn't have confusion or doubt that might lead to its changing its residence.

Their ears were pinned back as it was going to be dark, and they waited in ambush, holding their breath, Kodanddi with his loaded gun and Kothumban aiming with his tightly strung bows and newly sharpened arrows.

They were silent but vigilant. The moments were endless. The creatures of nature had their ways. The porcupines went out of their burrows after dusk but not too late and returned to the cave in the early hours of the day before the first rays of the sun awakened the sleeping earth. Their patience ended.

Lighting the lamp, Kodanddi made the call, "Sh... Sh...."

They got up. The porcupine had left earlier; perhaps it might have changed its dwelling or was already poached by others.

"Let's go," Kodanddi said. He seemed to be impatient, for he knew his mother's mood.

"Eager to reach home?" Kothumban said with a smile.

"You go away, lad," Kodanddi said, pretending to be angry.

Kothumban, who knew his moods, said, "Earlier, we spent nights together in the woods."

"My father was alive then. He looked after the family but now...."

Before Kodanddi could finish, Kothumban said, "You are married."

It was darker, and they couldn't see each other. The porcupine hasn't turned up.

"It's time that it came," the master said.

And in the dark woods amidst the chafers and millipedes, they waited for the sneaking return from its hideout. But it seemed that it would never turn up.

While the poachers retreated, disappointed, a feeling of missing haunted them.

Lighting the lamp, Kothumban walked ahead, and Kodanddi followed with arms and ammunition, talking little on the way.

Vellachi and Kasthuri waited for them. They felt no ill will or contempt, as they usually would, but said lovingly to go in for supper after the ablutions, for it was too late, especially for the forest dwellers.

"Where were you?" Kasthuri said with a smile.

"In the woods," said Kothumban. He was shy but glanced at her through the corner of his eyes.

Adjusting the upper cloth in the right position, which was forbidden to Vellachi, she said, "Didn't you learn from experience?"

Her look was penetrating and made him visibly shrink, but he said, "You like meat? Don't you, Thamburatty?"

"Yeah!" She nodded her head and said, "But…."

"We hunt in the woods for meat," Kothumban made it clear. Kodanddi was waiting for him to go to the rivulet.

Kasthuri was thoughtful. She knew nothing about poaching. But she said, "Going out in the woods at night is risky."

"When should we go hunting? You command Thamburatty," Kothumban said. She knew that he was mocking her.

She was perplexed. She knew he is normally obedient and always pleasant. But his little bit of arrogance made her unhappy.

But their stomach was fuming with hunger, and needed something instantly.

No sooner had they performed their ablutions than Vellachi served them supper.

The wild root, when peeled, looked bloody reddish but tasted differently. When munched, the juicy, fatty fluid filled their mouths, which they gulped hungrily.

Chapter 7

A few weeks passed by without anything special happening. The peasants came in dribs and drabs. The new rice boiled in new earthen vessels spreading its fragrance was stimulating. The weather was also fine, pleasant and sunny. The splendid harvest made the peasants rejoice under the cool shades of the green trees of the wood, singing and dancing.

The rivulet flowed down and swirled its rhythm as if in a procession celebrating victory. The youngsters spent most of their time swinging on the blossom vines or bathing in the waterfalls howling boisterously. In the meantime, they dug for wild roots or collected wild fruits and honey.

Women picked up fallen gooseberries, which had abundantly fallen to the ground. After cleansing and drying in the sun, the gooseberry would be put in the earthen jar filled with honey. Tightening the lids, these jars would be buried down in the earth for four to six months, making the content a rich nutrient, especially for children.

Some collected Hydnocarpus pentandra seeds or caster seeds; oil could be extracted, crushing them, mixing with water and boiling them for a long time, evaporating the water content completely. They would do the extraction, in which all the families would participate, and oil for the whole year would be obtained.

Occasionally men hunted in the woods, and they could often snare reddish deer or shoot bison or wild boars and spend their nights in revelry. On such nights it seemed that the hootch from all the villages couldn't quench their thirst. The men would behave as gluttons and would continue till the wee hours of the morning.

Those leisurely days were extremely fascinating to Kodanddi and Kasthuri. The colourfully blossomed vine thicket, fragrant and intoxicating, adorned their bridal chamber ostensibly, and they enjoyed the tumultuous pleasure of revellings. Together they swung in the flowery vines and took bath in the crystal clear and cool stream. Wild fruits and wild honey increased their fuddle. Kodanddi felt her skin smoother and fairer. Of course, she has become more beautiful.

One afternoon they were lying in the vine thicket, and Kodanddi said to her, "You feel a loss?"

"Never, my dear," her voice trickled down as honey drops.

"As a part of a wild tribe, now you lie in this thicket," he said as if he wanted to look into her mind.

"But it is smoother than the silk mattress I once had," she said softly.

It seemed to him that she didn't care about her loss, and her oomph has increased. Dipping the ripe figs in honey, he fed her. Her lips were ruby red.

"It's more than anything," she warbled.

"What?" he said, ogling her.

"Your love and care," she said. He has an unblemished mind, she thought.

"A princess in the woods," Kodanddi murmured. "You love the people, don't you?" she said.

"Oh! Yes," he responded.

"And you strive for them too?" she glanced at him.

"Not always," he said.

"But?"

"When it is necessary," he said reluctantly.

They blushed at the red blaze of the evening sky.

"You have won many adventurous deeds, haven't you?" she then said, complimenting him.

He hummed. He didn't say anything but looked at her. "You are brave. Mother has told me a lot."

"What?"

"About your deeds."

"They are my mother's dispositions," he said emotionlessly.

"Not at all. You possess princely dispositions." Her eulogizing words didn't excite him.

"What I do have is inherited from my father." His words were blunt. Engaging in love play, they spent a lot of time until it was dark.

Vellachi cast her eyes on them when they strolled back but didn't say anything. She came nearer to pick out the entangled dry leaves in her hair.

Supper, as usual, was delicious and plentiful. Boiled rice and stew made of wild roots along with roasted pork and condiment.

No one spoke. But everyone was thankful to Vellachi for the delicious meal she had prepared.

Once in bed, they embraced. "You are a true prince," she said lovingly to him. He hugged her warmly.

The consumption of sumptuous food, besides the languor of the day, made her fall fast asleep.

In the morning, Kasthuri felt giddiness, and Vellachi saw her vomiting under a jack fruit tree. She ran to her and caressed her back, for she knew it was a pregnancy symptom. She felt extremely happy. She led her to the cot, wiped her face and gave her water to drink.

Leaving her to take rest, Vellachi went back to the kitchen to mark the day as something special to be celebrated. But first he should make Kasthuri comfortable. Accordingly, she plucked a piece of green ginger. Cleansing it thoroughly, she crushed it with salty gooseberry and sliced coconut, adding a small pungent chilly to it.

Then she made millet porridge, serving it on a platter she called Kasthuri to come and eat. Hearing no response, she took the platter and went to chayippu.

Kasthuri hadn't overcome the giddiness. She was still lying half-fainted. Vellachi made her sit. Her eyes were still half closed; she wiped her face with a wet cloth. Using a spoon made of jack fruit tree leaves, she tried to feed her bit by bit.

"Gulp it, my dear," Vellachi lovingly said.

"I feel like retching, Mom," Kasthuri said. Her voice was so feeble and tired.

"You seem to be tired, my child." Vellachi's voice was encouraging. Kasthuri relented reluctantly to it.

She couldn't ignore her loving inducement. She gulped two or three spoons of porridge with some condiment.

But she tossed her cookies in double. She could not stop it from coming. Vellachi was worried. She rushed to inform her son, who was still lying asleep in sweet languor.

She could not wake her son fully, as he was in deep sleep and only make mild sounds when she called him.

"Oh! My son, wake up. Kasthuri is vomiting. She is exhausted," Vellachi said at the top of her voice.

But he paid no heed. He was still half asleep.

She shook him repeatedly and said, "Wake up, my son, Kasthuri is vomiting."

"Vomiting?" He expressed disbelief.

Then he said, "What have you given to her?" Kodanddi seemed to be querulous, or he mightn't have got the idea.

"Why is she vomiting?" He looked at his mother.

"Oh! I don't know." smiling at him meaningfully, she turned away.

Kodanddi went into the chayippu. He saw Kasthuri lying exhausted. He sat beside her and caressed her forehead lovingly.

He put her head on his lap, and without bothering about the roughness of his palm, he caressed her.

"Now I feel secure in your hands," she said feebly to him.

"You must eat and drink well," he said to her.

"But I feel a numbness in my head," she said.

"It is because of nausea, I think," he said, wiping her lips with a wet cloth.

He went to the kitchen and brought some fruit pulp in a bowl. Scooping it with a leaf spoon, he dripped it in her mouth. She gulped three or four spoonfuls. Then she said, "Enough."

"You take rest; I'm going out."

"Don't be too late, I'm afraid," she said in a sinking voice.

The giddiness and nausea came morning after morning. It seemed that it would never stop. She became leaner and leaner day by day. Vellachi seemed troubled in her mind.

She said to her son to take Kasthuri to a green herb physician.

Kasthuri was too weak to walk. Accordingly, a litter was to be made to carry her to the herbal physician residing a dozen miles away through a forest footpath with a lot of hills and dales.

Kothumban and three others came and made a temporary palanquin. They were to start early the next morning.

The hilly, slippery path was perilous and carrying the palanquin seemed risky. Two carried the litter on their shoulders, chanting, "hoi... hoi...." Two walked ahead carrying sticks and choppers as guards. Kodanddi walked behind, carrying a bow pendant on his left shoulder and a loaded gun on his right. The litter bearers and guards were changed in turn; many times, they had to stop to clear the way.

However, they reached the physician before noon. The old dark man with grey-white hair and beard was grinding some herbal medicines to make pills. He looked curiously at them when they placed the litter on the verandah of his house. As Kasthuri emerged out of the litter, lightning flashed through the bearded man's face, and he looked at her from top to bottom.

The physician had spotted Kasthuri as soon as he saw her but said nothing. He pretended that he didn't know her. Instructing others to sit, the prescient physician moved to her for consultation, examined her pulse using his thumb and examined her eyes and tongue. He then examined her lower abdomen, and he said, "Nothing to worry about; she's pregnant." Then he cast his eyes on Kodanddi.

"She's vomiting incessantly," Kodanddi said.

"It's quite natural. It'll be reduce after a few weeks. She'll be all right then. You take these pills and green herb decoction one ounce twice a day, after mixing the pill in it." The physician said.

"For how many days?" Kodanddi said.

"For one week," the physician said.

Then he handed over the pills and the bottle of decoction.

Kodanddi gave him two silver coins. At first, he was reluctant to accept them, but on compulsion, he accepted with much reluctance and appeared not pellucid or preternatural.

The physician didn't forget to give them food and drink before they left. They have to reach home before dark. So, hurriedly they resumed their journey, wasting no time.

They feared animal attacks, but there were no issues or any misfortune on the way.

They reached home safely before dark.

But a mysterious fear began to trouble Kasthuri. Sometimes it might be her fear or something more than that. Yet her fear took shape and grew monstrously. She was totally confined to her bed with pills and decoctions. Sometimes it seemed that she even feared her own shadow.

Vellachi gave offerings to the gods of the mountain to cast off her fears. The rustling of the leaves, the climbing of the lizards or the movement of the chameleons would often terrify her. She would shudder when human footsteps were heard.

"What makes you so frightened?" Kodanddi said to her one day after seeing her shudder.

She didn't want to destroy his peace of mind. Let him have his sleep, she thought. She shook her head but decided to disclose it to him at the appropriate time.

Chapter 8

Vellachi was weeding out colocasia, bending too low, her dangling breasts almost touching the ground. Kodanddi had been out into the woods to check the snares he had put out the previous day.

Vellachi heard human voices completely unfamiliar to her. Straightening her back, she looked around and saw two men standing in her courtyard, watching the house seriously. From their conversation, she conjectured that they were the henchmen from the *Kovilakam*. She tremored and was struck still, like a statue that couldn't move or speak for a long time.

Slowly she took the sickle and walked to the courtyard shivering and panting and stood in front of them, showing reverence.

"You reside here?" one of them said to her.

"Who else is with you?" the other said. They were watching her closely.

Words wouldn't come out of her. She was terribly frightened. At last, she stammered out as though she had a lump in her throat. "My... son... and his wife."

"Where are they?" they said together in one voice.

"In the woods," she muttered, shivering.

"For what?" The questions seemed never to cease. "Digging... digging for roots," she said in a hurry.

"When will they come back?" was the next query.

In the meantime, she had gathered some courage; otherwise,

it might have crushed her heart.

"Before dark," she said.

"A princess won't go digging in the woods," one of them inferred.

"Then it might not be the princess," the other said.

The men looked at each other, and sensing no malice, turned to go.

Before leaving, one of them uttered, "We're looking for a princess."

"A princess! That too in the forest!" Vellachi exclaimed.

"Yeah! An outcast who wedded into a wild tribe," they said, showing their contempt.

"It's heard that she's residing somewhere here. We are looking for her." The man from the *Kovilakam* said. Only then did the calamity awaiting them dawn on her and her heart sank for a while.

She didn't offer them food or drink for fear that they might stay long or be concerned that they wouldn't eat from a tribe woman. But as a courtesy, she offered buttermilk to them. They nodded their heads.

She went in and asked Kasthuri to go out into the woods through the back door and hide in the woods until the King's men went. Then she took the buttermilk in an earthen jar and placed it before them.

It was appropriately mixed with salt and green chilly and flavoured with pomegranate leaves. They drank and quenched their thirst.

"We'll have to find her wherever she is," one of the men said.

"Oh! We forgot to look inside," the other said suspiciously.

"What a grave mistake!" exclaimed the other.

"We can't miss her," the former said. Together they entered

the hut to search, and having found no one, they quit.

After some time, Vellachi called Kasthuri out from her hiding place behind a bush. She had become totally pale.

"You are terribly frightened," said Vellachi. It seemed that she would groan like a frightened animal trapped by the tiger and retreated to the rear. Kasthuri entered the chayippu. She was sobbing when Vellachi came in.

She had a handful of salt, small pungent chilly and mustard seed in her right palm. Closing her fingers tightly, she made a circling movement with her right palm around Kasthuri's head three times and put them in the burning coal at the fireplace. It was to cast off the fright in her. They cracked in low sounds.

"Didn't you hear the cracking?" Vellachi said to her. "The evil spirits have gone. So cheer up my Thamburatty Kutty," she looked at her. The word Thamburatty suddenly penetrated her heart all the more severe, like a thorn than the presentiment. It was causing trouble for her.

"Can't you exempt the word 'Thamburatty'?" Kasthuri said to Vellachi.

"Why should I? It gives me some honour," Vellachi said, looking at her with a smile.

"Then it's a word of misfortune." Her words were all soaked in self-contempt.

"No, it's a word of fortune," Vellachi dared to deny her princess.

"You see," she began to explain, "We reaped a rich harvest when you stepped in. Kodanddi is honoured among the tribes. It's because of you. What else?" Vellachi was all praise for her son.

"He is a very good farmer. Besides, he helps others," Kasthuri babbled. "These qualities were in him earlier, too," she added.

"But he didn't get any honour. Now things have changed because of you," Vellachi said.

Kasthuri was astonished over her power of assimilation.

"But I have no power. I have no kingdom or force. These have been taken away from me." Kasthuri seemed frustrated and helpless.

"You will get them back soon. The knights have come especially for you," Vellachi was optimistic.

"No, Mom. They have come to present my head on a platter to Vasundhara." Vellachi had never seen her so upset.

"Let it come as the mountain Gods decide," she said to Vellachi and left the kitchen. Meanwhile, Kodanddi returned from the woods along with Kothumban carrying the carcass of a porcupine.

After removing the quills, they peeled its skin. Then they tore its stomach with a dagger and removed the intestine, and washed it thoroughly before they cut it into small pieces. Sharing the meat into two, Kothumban left taking one share. Kodanddi took the other and placed it in the kitchen.

A totally disturbed Vellachi moved to the kitchen, her heart throbbing. She had become silent, eyes turbid and cheeks swelled.

Seeing her like this, Kodanddi said, "Mom, you look sad. What makes you so gloomy?"

"We may lose Kasthuri, I'm afraid," she said, sobbing.

"Miss her? How?" Kodanddi could not believe her words.

Anxiously she said, "Two henchmen have come from the palace." Her voice was trembling.

"Did they see her?" Kodanddi asked.

"No, I had sent her to the hideout in the bush before they

entered." She was boastful of her tricks.

"What did they say?" Kodanddi said.

"They wanted the princess."

"Were they after her?"

"Oh! Sure! They said that they would have to find the princess at any cost," she said.

"Then they'll come again," he said, taking a deep breath.

Why they had come puzzled him. He sweated and got exhausted severely. His body seemed to stink after the butchery. He went to the rivulet for a bath, taking the Acacia intsia scrubber.

Vellachi began to cook the meat for lunch. Porcupine meat would taste slightly bitter even if it was spiced well. Kasthuri wouldn't eat it for fear of nausea caused by the bitterness of the meat. But Vellachi liked it.

The villagers should be alerted about the visit of the King's men to the hillock, Kodanddi thought. Otherwise, the news about Kasthuri may leak out. The innocent peasants would disclose when questioned, being unaware of the frightful consequences.

Challenging the scorching sun, he set out. The seriousness of the threat had put him on red alert and made him visit each and every hut in the village to ask his fellow men not to disclose that she was there. People were ready to throw in their lot with him, yet he remained sceptical, fearing the extreme efforts by the King's couriers. The thoughts began to crush his mind. He must make a secret hideout readily accessible neither to the foe nor his fellow men, but it should be far away from his home. He scoured all the forests nearby up and down north, south, east, and west until he finally spotted an ideal place.

It was on the bank of a rivulet, a flat-surfaced rock almost covered with trees. It would be the rendezvous for them during the daytime. A sloped ladder was to be made to access the smooth surface of the rock top.

Autumn was coming to an end. The winter would come next, and there would be no rain for the coming two or three months. Then there would be a sudden outbreak of summer. Showers with thunder and lightning. Somehow he would have to take the plunge.

A roof atop the rock would make it easily identifiable. Frequently there would be spies of the queen roaming or betrayers among his fellow men. Kodanddi couldn't think of any loophole.

Then he thought of a cave on the other side of the hillock, but it seemed a precarious hideaway to him, with frequent visits of tigers or reptiles making the hideaway more perilous than the swords of the King's men.

He heard the growling of the tiger at a distance. The dusk was to come, covering the hillock with a dark woollen blanket. Hearing the growling, a herd of elks fled. Kodanddi took his country gun and began to load it slowly.

Vellachi nursed Kasthuri in the chayippu. She combed her hair and made her dress in fresh clothes. The fret and panic of pregnancy had subsided to an extent, and a pale smile spread on her face.

Kodanddi told his mother to latch the door firmly. Taking his gun, he went out and took position on the top of a rock which he thought would be an ideal spot.

Listening to the stir, he aimed with his right hand on the trigger, ready to shoot at any time. If not, he could jump on the other side of the rock and escape.

Suddenly he heard a movement at a distance; holding his breath, he aimed. He could see its glowing eyes and fairly big head.

He assumed that it would be a large, fierce animal. His heart began to beat faster, and his knees trembled. Yet he controlled himself. He was at its leap's length away, but it seemed to be confused on whether to or not.

Aiming at the back of the left ear, he pulled the trigger. The gun went off, booming, and echoed on the hillock several times. The animal turned around and fell down with a fierce cry.

Hearing the gun go off, people came running with shouts and arms waving. "Don't go near. It's not dead," Kodanddi warned them.

A large animal striped in black and brown lay on its side, its head in a pool of blood, still breathing. Standing on the top of the rock, Kodanddi was loading his gun again as if a second shot was necessary.

People were cheering. Some were enthusiastic about touching the animal, and a few wanted to pull its tail. But Kodanddi went on cautioning them.

"It will rise and scratch with its claws," he warned, but they were too enthusiastic to hear his words.

Kothumban took a wooden staff and tried to make the animal lie on its back. Suddenly the animal rose and, sitting on its posterior, seized Kothumban and embraced him, fiercely digging its claws deep into his back before he could do anything.

He was shocked and uttered, "*Ayyo… Ayyo…*" and writhed in pain. People fled in different directions, screaming. Some climbed on trees, and some even on Coral trees. Before Kodanddi came down, the animal loosened its grasp and fell on its back dead.

Kothumban's back was bleeding. Kodanddi carried him home, gave him water to drink, cleaned his wounds and applied the sap of *Folia Malabathy* on them. Kothumban writhed and wriggled in pain and groaned.

Soon after, many people who met with cuts and bruises while fleeing came. Having nursed them, they were sent to their homes.

"What do we do with the carcass?" someone said.

"Bury it. What else?" young and enthusiastic Veluthu said.

"Before that, we will have to remove its skin and nails." The middle-aged Karuthumbu, who always had a commercial outlook, said.

"We'll have to carry the carcass to the *Adhikari*[46]," Kodanddi said.

"What for?" Veluthu asked querulously.

"To cut out its tongue." Veluthu thought it was so queer. The nincompoop didn't grasp the idea.

"It can be done here," was his surmise.

"No, my lad, it should be cut in the presence of the *Adhikari*," Kodanddi explained.

"Is it medicinal? Veluthu was ardent.

"If it is, we'll preserve it," Karuthumbu supported.

"No, it's highly poisonous," said Kodanddi.

"Who told you?" was his query.

"My father told me." Nobody could repudiate Kodanddi's father, Chavanian.

"Then what shall we do with it?" Karuthumbu expressed his undue haste.

"It should be burnt to ashes." Kodanddi had a clear vision.

"Then?"

"The ashes should be dissolved in a large quantity of water and be poured into the soil," Kodanddi said.

---

[46] A village officer.

"Why so much caution?" Veluthu again said.

"If it is not destroyed, it can be misused." Kodanddi looked at his face, and Veluthu nodded his head as a mark of conviction. It had become dark. But they couldn't wait for daybreak for the carcass might ruin.

Men set off immediately with arms and lights, carrying the carcass pendant on a wooden staff.

Vellachi sighed in relief. The youngsters were eager to get its nails which could be hung from their necks as an ornament and would be marked as a sign of bravery. The skin could be dried and spread on the wall of the house as a mark of valour of the archer. The village waited anxiously for the return of the carcass.

Chapter 9

"You become a peahen, and I'll be your peacock," Kodanddi said to Kasthuri.

It was one pleasant evening. They were taking rest on the rock-top in the woods. "Agreed," she said, glancing at him. Her cheek blushed.

The reddened sun lit up the woods in amazing colours. She seemed to be aroused.

Stepping down from the rock-top, they began to dance. The sun permeated through the green thickets and spotted them in colours.

Rubbing their beaks, they expressed their love. "I'll give you a kiss. Can I have your lips, honey?" The peacock pecked at his hen.

Pecking back, the peahen said, "You can nibble an ocean of honey."

"Can I have the warmth of your breast?" Pressing his chest upon her and joining their beaks together, the peacock whispered.

"You take the warmth when the mist showers." The peahen warbled.

Biting one end of a fig, the peacock placed the other end to the peahen's beak.

"Will the honey make it sweeter?" the peacock said.

"Your love is sweeter than the honey," The peahen rendered softly.

When Kodanddi embraced her closely, she said, "You know

I am carrying? So go slowly," she said softly and swooned.

The peahen felt the heat of his passion and was aroused. The gentle breeze showered flowers on them. It carried pollen grain and fragrance.

They danced hand in hand, making each step spontaneous and rhythmic, escorted by the music of the cuckoo. The sounds of the waterfall thrilled them.

Caressing her, he said, "This landscape is beautiful."

"And so cool," she said.

"Your presence makes it more beautiful," he then said.

"Your love makes it sweeter." Her words were sweeter than the honey.

Swinging and singing, they moved on. The slushy green thicket fanned them softly. The warbling of the birds accompanied.

The setting sun began to sink on the other side of the hillock. Before it grew dark, they returned.

Vellachi was waiting for them with steaming rice gruel and condiments.

"You have been too far. You are tired," Vellachi said.

"What can we do, Mom, if the knights come again?" Kodanddi said, looking at her.

There was silence. They were wracking their brains for a solution. "It's better to keep away," Vellachi suggested.

"Keep away?" Kodanddi knitted his eyebrows.

"Yeah! You keep away in the woods," she said.

"But how long?" Kodanddi again raised his brows.

"Until their real intention is revealed," Vellachi said. It seemed to be a wise advice.

Kasthuri had a shy smile over it. She looked at him sideways through the corner of her eyes.

Though they were enjoying their hideout, he was to bring about its inevitability.

The hot rice gruel made them sweat.

"Don't drink it too hot," Vellachi advised Kasthuri. "It'll affect the child," she explained.

Kasthuri looked at her in amazement. She was astonished over the tribal woman's practical wisdom.

Even late at night, Vellachi kept a vigilant ear, and she had sleepless nights. "What would we do if the King's men came at night?" she asked herself. It seemed to trouble her all the more. "Let the Gods of the mountain protect them," she sighed. It was long and deep. She tossed and turned all night. Sometimes she had nightmares.

Day after day, Kasthuri and Kodanddi spent their days in the woods, and the pregnancy caused her stomach to swell.

In the meantime, the knights had visited the hillock two or three times but could not trace the princess's presence.

For a long time, there were no visits, and it seemed that they had given up.

"The ruler watches and waits for the right time," Kasthuri observed.

"Spies are the ruler's eyes," said Kodanddi regarding the absence of the knights' visits. Kasthuri knew for certain the King's ways.

The seventh month of her pregnancy had begun. She was at her '*Nei-seva*[47]'. She had become fat but pale.

Every morning she went for a walk along with Vellachi, usually on the plains avoiding steep hillocks. Every afternoon she

---

[47] The consumption of ghee by the pregnant woman.

bathed in warm water, smearing gingelly oil all over her body. This was to make the delivery easy and without exertion. Vellachi helped her by smearing oil on her back before bath. Kodanddi had gone in search of a midwife in a faraway village. Offering gold and silver sovereigns in addition to grains as quid-pro-quo for her service, he brought her weeks before the actual date of delivery. As it was a royal birth, precautional measures would be taken to ensure everything was in order. They didn't want to take any risk.

Spotting the incongruency, the midwife began to ask questions to identify her clan before she took charge.

But Kasthuri, being strategical, only told her that she had been expelled from a royal family and had been abandoned in the woods to die and rescued by Kodanddi. Since then, she has been living with him; he had given her care and protection. She couldn't find any reason not to choose him as her life partner.

"But you have a name," the serpent-eyed midwife said.

"Kasthuri," she said as coolly as she could.

The midwife observed her with her serpent eyes. She didn't ask further queries but began contemplating her own navel. Clad in white, the midwife looked fair even in her late fifties. Her hair had not become too white and skin not wrinkled, and she possessed a serious look.

Three times Vellachi had intervened. But Kasthuri's gestures prevented her from saying anything, which Kasthuri feared would be risking her hideout. She offered ornaments to the midwife if she attended well to her delivery, and nursed her after that.

The midwife seemed to be satisfied and took over Kasthuri's charge.

Vellachi was much relieved and thereafter paid her full

attention in the kitchen. She had already made gruel with bran-rice. She crushed dried wild boar's meat to make the relish. Then she made the ginger chutney and mixed it with curd.

They sat down for their early supper. The gruel and relish went well. The midwife, too, ate well.

Kasthuri asked for her name.

"Manikyam, Mali Manikyam," her voice was full of pride.

Finishing the gruel, she washed her platter and hands. Then she sat on a mat and demanded chewing pan. Vellachi brought the betel box to her. She chewed lavishly and spat in the courtyard keeping her two fingers across her lips. Then she began to boast about her feats as a midwife. Kasthuri and Vellachi listened to her.

"You need good sleep," Manikyam said. "A pregnant woman should not be deprived of sleep," she explained.

Kasthuri retired to the chayippu.

"You too can sleep in the chayippu," Vellachi said to Manikyam.

A bed was arranged especially for her in the chayippu. Manikyan, being treated as a distinguished guest, felt very proud. She was expecting a little fortune, too, for her endeavour. So she reminded them about sacrifice frequently.

"I usually don't stay long," she said. "But it is for you. I couldn't turn a deaf ear to his words."

"We know," Kasthuri said. "We value your sacrifice."

"That's enough," Manikyam made a contented laugh. Kasthuri felt she was bossy.

Kodanddi had become a bundle of nerves. Though he performed his duties well, he was disturbed by thoughts. The King's men definitely must be keeping their eagle eyes on the tribes.

The hostile Mannanar was looking for a chance to crush the tribals who he had been at loggerheads with for years over the arrears of land tenancy. Besides, Kodanddi was a thorn in his side. Hootch was in full flow, and his men were sinking in it. They had even lost their interest in farming, spent most of their time hunting wild boars or bison, and were content with the abundant meat.

Kodanddi feared that his men would become flotsam and jetsam. Their virility should be brought back, he thought. He had often gone with the flow so as not to be isolated. He remembered his father saying, "Nearby foes are better benefactors than far away relatives."

Kodanddi couldn't sleep well that night. Yet he got up early. He wanted to go to the hill tract at day break. For several months they had been playing peacock and hen in the woods. The sweet memory still prevailed in him. It's high time that the work started for the next season's paddy.

Kodanddi called out Kothumban and others. Kothumban has not been free of his hangover yet and made excuses. Karuthu and Veluthu were ready to go with him. Later, Karuthumbu also joined them on the hill tract.

It was a landscape almost covered by the creepers of Acasia intsia. The creepers had squeezed and terminated other small plants and weeds, barring, a few alata trees and a large knotty tree, Laurus cassia.

"It will be very difficult to cut Intsia," said Veluthu with a look of disgust on his face.

"But the land is so fertile," said Karuthu.

"The soil is very mature," said Veluthu.

"And easy to scoop," said Karuthu.

The white flowers of thorny Intsia laughed mocking at the

men. No wild animal had dared to enter that part of the land, fearing its thorns. But they are not aware of the diligence of man. The Laurus cassia pervaded its fragrance everywhere with its flowers and leaves.

"We needn't chop the knotty tree. It's beautiful and fragrant," Kodanddi said.

"We can rest under its cool shade," said Veluthu, who liked leisurely hours.

"The soil with Intsia would be so fertile. We can reap two hundred measures," boasted Karuthumbu.

Everyone agreed to stop for the time being and decided to return with sharp choppers and sickles early the next morning.

Like fishing hooks, intsia hooked up into their flesh, and most of them complained about the severe pain. Their hands were inflamed. The sweat made it all the more severe, yet they didn't give up. In the scorching sun, they quenched their thirst by drinking water flavoured with the essence of sarsaparilla.

Karuthumbu cracked jokes to ease their toil and pain. Young women with unveiled breasts shyly concealed their laughter. The bashfulness made them more beautiful. Their breasts bobbed, and cheeks blushed.

Looking at Kurinchi, Veluthu sipped concocter from pot gourd. After a short break, they resumed their work with increased vigour. The rest and joviality had eased away their tiredness and pain.

Seeing Kodanddi silent and gloomy, Karuthumbu attacked him with his humour. "You are afraid of losing your royal wife?"

Kodanddi, alarmed, looked at him and said, "You are fit to be a clown."

"I will be when your wife becomes the queen." he retaliated quickly. It was near the knuckle. Kodanddi sighed as though he was alarmed.

In the middle of the afternoon, the men sat under the knotty tree and the women under the Euginia Recemose nearby for privacy.

Cracking jokes, they drank the previous day's rice gruel from the bottle gourd tasting condiments. They exchanged drinks. Karuthumbu cracked jokes, and all the seven men burst into laughter while the women, six in number, were engaged in gossip.

Veluthu had brought fried stag's meat, which he gave away to all in common gum tree leaves.

"You got so much of elk's meat?" said Karuthu.

"The hunters gave me some. The antler was a big one," explained Veluthu.

While giving the meat to Kurinchi, his hands shook. She glanced at him, smiling. Veluthu wished they were alone under the cool shade of Racemose. He looked at her longingly. Though not the belle of the ball, her pretty blushed cheeks and those two fairly round 'anars' made him love-stricken.

He could have fondled her. He wished there was a speedy sunset or a sudden solar eclipse.

Seeing them love-stricken, Karuthumbu remarked, "*Kurinchikku thalayum mulayum vanna pinne penninu chekkane thedante?*"[48]

"*Chekkan ibide thane undu*[49]," Narayani said.

Everyone burst into laughter. Veluthu and Kurinchi were shrinking with bashfulness. The love birds chirped in the Euginia Racemose, marking the end of the day. The gentle breeze

---

[48] Kurinchi has become a youthful girl. Her hair and breast have become robust. It is time to seek a bridegroom.
[49] The bridegroom is here itself.

caressed them with coolness and wiped off their sweat. The fragrance filled their nostrils.

When the evening's red blaze spread over the west, the men and women were on their way home. The birds had begun to perch in their nests. The reptiles moved towards the water-brook to quench their thirst. A multitude of storks flew towards the north.

Carrying the heavy chopper, Kodanddi walked towards his home with firm footsteps and a heavy heart.

Nothing untoward had happened, as he feared it would. Vellachi was combing her niece's hair. The midwife was smearing '*Kuzhambu*' on Kasthuri; Manikyam preferred to smear 'Kuzhambu' on her inner thigh and loins, saying it would ease delivery. The trio talked incessantly.

Manikyam took Kasthuri for a small walk before she took her to bathe in the warm *vethu*. They were careful not to go near the Alstonia Scholaris tree, believed to be the home of a fairy.

Vellachi had told her many fairy tales. The fairy had charmed and tempted many youths with her beauty, seduced and killed them, sucking their blood. There remained their hairs and skeletons under the tree for many days, Vellachi had said. As the days went by the serious concern over the security of Kasthuri grew into terrible anxiety and alarm.

Though Kodanddi worked on the hill tract along with the others, his mind was fully at home. Only his body was there. The hooking up of the Intsia was less severe than the hooking up in his heart. He expected the King's men at any time.

Chapter 10

It was on the tenth day of Medam, the auspicious day for farmers, and Kodanddi and the other tribesmen would sow seeds in the hill tract. All the men had come with implements early. Kodanddi had prepared the seeds ready to sow. They had decided to sow '*Pannikuttan*' that year.

He took six '*Pothis*[50]' of '*Pannikuttan*[51]' seeds from inside and mixed them with dhal gram seeds. Seeds of Pumpkin and Cucumber were also added. Then they gathered it in the sacks and marched towards the hill tract carrying the sacks of seeds and small hoes.

Kothumban, who had at first abstained from chopping the hill tract, had come with increased vigour; others raised eyebrows at him. But he didn't care about them. Women followed them, carrying pot gourds filled with rice gruel. Some had brought condiments and others wild meat dishes. Women with their breastfeeding babies were also there.

It all looked like a pageantry of peasants with their kids and pets on a warm sunny morning.

Some tied cloth cradles in the Laurus cassia and some on the Euginia Racemose.

Having fed them milk, they laid them in the cradles.

The rustling of the leaves became a lullaby while the gentle wind swang the cradles. Two men sowed seeds while others tilled

---

[50] Bundles.
[51] A kind of paddy.

the rich soil bending with their hoes in rows.

Like the waves in the sea advanced towards the shore, the rows advanced with their hoes putting their best-foot forward.

They forgot everything, even their kids sleeping in the cradles. The scorching sun above them had made the soil below too hot. They sweated and panted. The soil and the ashes of the burnt thick vegetations gave a coating to their bodies. More than half of the land had been tilled before they took their midday meal.

Before resuming the sowing and tilling, mothers fed their kids and left them in the cradles so that they could work without interruption. Karuthumbu's jokes were risible and sometimes vulgar when they fell into obscene. Anyhow it eased their worries and pain. They had to toil hard to till the entire land before the sunset.

The whole party proceeded to their homes then; the men carrying their tools and the women with their kids and pets.

"Take bath; otherwise you will be stuck together," said Karuthumbu.

Everyone laughed. Thinking upon its depth, Kodanddi couldn't help but laugh. The gratification of the work was not less than the stress of the toil, perhaps even higher.

The summer rain that night was kind and sufficient. It was neither too heavy nor too light. The seeds, along with the soil, would be washed away in the gushing water flow if it rained heavily, and the seeds wouldn't germinate if it was insufficient.

The smell of the fresh earth spread everywhere when it rained, enthusing the hearts of the couples to get united.

The shower subsided. The cool wind brought chilliness and gave consolation and pleasure to the peasants for the next few days.

The peasants planted tubular plants, colo cassia and elephant yam, in different plots. Some planted ginger and turmeric.

Kodanddi was spading up small platforms for planting ginger. He had already made several such platforms for turmeric and dug small pits in an array on them to plant the ginger pieces.

Vellachi scattered powdered dried cow dung on the platforms. Having put the seed pieces in the pits, she covered them with the soil. Then she made a thick coating for the platforms with green leaves.

Mali Manikyam has been sincerely attending on Kasthuri since she arrived. Vellachi was relieved since then so that she could help her son in farming.

The summer showers were adequate, and within a fortnight, the whole hill tract was covered with a green carpet. Frequent showers made it thicker and coloured the hopes of the peasants.

The green earth below, the blue sky above, and the blossomed laburnum and Racemose tree in between; Nature had showered its entire splendour upon the hillock.

In the evenings, they would sit in the open, enjoying the breeze while Manikyam led Kasthuri for a walk. Kodanddi felt pity for her. Her pregnancy was full, she looked weary, and her walking was affected. Her feet had swelled.

Manikyam said, "You are nearing the date. That's why you have this swelling."

"Any problem?" Kasthuri said

"Nothing," Manikyam said abruptly. "It's very common."

In the evening, Manikyam was massaging Kasthuri with '*Kuzhumbu*'[52]. She noted a lump on the right side of Kasthuri's stomach. Manikyam held her left palm upon it. She could feel the movement of the baby. Then she put her ear to her stomach. She

---

[52] The medicine oil.

could clearly hear the sound of the baby's movements. "It's a prince," Manikyam said.

"How could you know that?" Kasthuri said with a smile.

"Your stomach is tilted towards the right," Manikyam expressed her knowledge with pride.

The kicks and stamps in the womb has become so intense. Kasthuri enjoyed the movements with untold bliss.

One morning when Manikyam had gone to the toilet in the bush, Kasthuri called Kodanddi inside.

They were sleeping in separate rooms since Mali Manikyam came to nurse her. Since then, she has been missing his rough with gentle caresses. "I miss you a lot," she said.

"It's for your goodness," he said.

"My goodness is to be with you," she said with a little ill-will in her voice.

Then she asked him to put his ear to her stomach. He could hear the vigorous movement in the womb. He was thrilled with excitement. "He's active and energetic," he exclaimed.

"Like you?" she said with a smile.

He caressed her cheeks, moved his fingers through her hair and kissed her forehead. It filled her with eternal bliss. She closed her eyes in great rapture.

Mali Manikyam peeped into the room with a cough to make them alert to her presence. Kodanddi retreated to the raised bank in front of their home.

Vellachi was preparing broken rice porridge in the kitchen. She had told Kodanddi to drink some before leaving for the hill tract for his usual morning rounds. She served the steaming porridge on a platter. A pinch of salt was added. Using a ladle, she mixed it well. It was very hot. He drank it slowly.

The paddy had grown at least a foot in height, perhaps above their expectations. Each and every paddy plant had sprouted into hundreds making the cultivation dense. He doubted whether it had been sown thick. The fertile soil had converted the paddy plants into multitudes. No doubt there were fewer weeds.

The millet, too, had grown an inch taller, darker and greener, resembling the border of the scapular worn by the hillock.

The pumpkin and cucumber made dot-like marks on them. The Racemose and the laburnum embroidered gold.

Soon the wind began to blow. Knowing it to be the precursor of the southwest monsoon. Kodanddi hurried back home. Seeing the flourishing hill tract, he was extremely happy. Before the rains started, he would have to thatch his roof and store enough firewood, he thought.

They had an abundance of palm leaves. Kothumban and two others came early in the morning to start on the roofing. It all sounded easy as there was no damage to the rafters supporting the roof or the strips of bamboo.

Kasthuri and Mali Manikyam took rest under the ironwood tree. Vellachi cooked in the open space till the thatching was over.

She had made par-boiled rice porridge and yam stew and condiments for lunch. Dried stag's meat was also fried.

Plantain leaf stalk was placed curved as a base support and Plantain leaf was placed on it so that porridge wouldn't flow out. The sweet aroma of the plantain when the hot porridge was served added taste. On another leaf, the dishes were served. They had a hearty meal for lunch.

The firewood house was also to be thatched with palm leaves. They worked till the very red blaze of the sky magnificently crowned the hillock.

Kodanddi offered the men paddy, but they were reluctant to accept, saying that the work was voluntary as it used to be.

Thatching of house roofs used to be a village festival in which the young and old alike participated.

"Don't consider it as coolie or a free gift," Kodanddi said thoughtfully.

"It's our duty," Kothumban said.

"And mine too," said Kodanddi.

"You can take it if you have a deficit in paddy."

Kodanddi took a sack of paddy out from the inner room and gave it to Kothumban. "You share as you like."

Finally, they took the paddy hesitatingly and walked stealthily away. Taking the bath towel, Kodanddi went to the rivulet.

Water had diminished in the rivulet because of the summer heat. New springs would make it full when the monsoon thickens, and water would flow down heavily.

The cool water refreshed his body as well as his mind.

On his return, he heard the women quarrelling loudly. He couldn't pass by without listening. "Scores of heads can unite, but can't four breasts?" he thought. When he came close, he learned that the families of Veluthu and Kurinchi were arguing.

Kurinchi had eloped with Veluthu to the nearby woods in the morning and had not yet returned. Kurinchi's family had been searching for her since then. They reached the residence of Veluthu and demanded her return immediately.

When denied they had almost come to blows with each other, a hot exchange of words continued.

"Where's Kurinchi?" her mother demanded. Having no response from Veluthu's house, she raised her voice, "What did you do with her?"

"You should have brought her up with more control?" Veluthu's mother said. The remark raised the opponent's rage.

"You harlot, what did you say? How many times have you defied your husband?" Veluthu's father, who was standing nearby, became infuriated and came forward and said, "*Muthukki,* you say vagary?"

"What vagary? Your son seduced my daughter," Kurinchi's mother retaliated.

"Your daughter's fuddle seduced my son," Veluthu's mother alleged.

"Oh! A chaste woman has come!" she ridiculed. "Then you lick his…"

"Nobody ever said a word about my son," Velutha's mother claimed. "He's a simpleton."

"Pooh! Simpleton!" Kurinchi's mother forced up the phlegm and spat wildly, and alleged, "He leers at women's behinds."

"Only you said it, gold digger," Veluthu's mother retaliated.

"You wheedled money?" Kurinchi's mother said

Both families uttered vulgar and obscene words at each other.

"What the fuck? You looked for bigger… to satisfy your lust," Veluthu's mother's rage rose like a flaming fire. "Oh! You forgot everything. I still remember," she said.

"What the hell do you remember? You rogue?" Kurinchi's mother said.

"Your quagmire, you don't force me to say more," Veluthu's mother said in a threatening tone.

"What do you want to say, you voyeur?" Raising her voice, Kurinchi's mother shouted.

"Your wailing. What else?" Veluthu's mother was not ready to withdraw. "Your mother-in-law poured pepper soup on your posteriors."

It was the ultimate weapon to be used against her. Kurinchi's mother retreated in full cry.

Kurinchi's father, who was standing calmly by, came forward and said to his wife, "Didn't you get enough?"

"Your forearm isn't stout. Otherwise, you would have questioned it," she said to him. The remark seemed to question his virility and infuriated him. He advanced with her uncle.

Thinking that he had come to attack them, Veluthu's father bawled at them, "You cunnilingus bull. What do you want?"

Sensing the danger, Kodanddi rushed in and stopped them.

"What nonsense is this?" he said. "Haven't you thought of your daughter bound to live with them?"

"You needn't pay heed to him; he's a consort," Kurinchi's mother insulted him.

"Then do what you wish. See what would come out of the skirmish," Kodanddi said. Hearing the pandemonium Kothumban and some others came running with sticks. The arguing families had to retreat to their houses, and the people had a good laugh over it and dispersed.

The dear and near ones waited for the lovers, burning the midnight oil. But they did not turn up. The arguments seemed to be a feigned quarrel to hoodwink the neighbours.

When everyone was asleep and the village plunged into silence in the wee hours of the morning, Veluthu crept into his house with Kurinchi through the kitchen door, which hadn't been locked, consumed the late supper waiting for them, and retired to their bedroom as they were exhausted with love-play.

That night there was much thunder and lightning, and the whistling wind brought chilliness, causing the lovers to cuddle closer, but when the golden beams of the sun awoke the hillock, everyone was quiet and happy. The drops of rain on the shrubs and plants smiled. The neighbours were astonished to see Veluthu and Kurinchi coming out of their thatched hut, gleaming as if they were stepping out of heaven into the world of realities.

Nobody came to question them. Her cheeks and lips seemed to blush. Though they had remained awake all night and rheum appeared in their eyes, they continued with their routine.

Kodanddi, as usual, had gone to the hill tract early in the morning. Vellachi had instructed him to come back as early as he could. She was worried about Kasthuri's delivery. Paddy had grown to knee-high, healthy and dark green. On the border, green millet had grown faster. It seemed to him that the paddy would blossom soon, shooting the tender spike as the footstalk of the plant had become thicker. "'*Pannikuttan*' would yield a rich harvest," he said to himself.

On his return, Kodanddi visited Veluthu's hut. He was sitting on the raised bank of his hut, waiting for breakfast. Kurinchi appeared with a platter full of steamed tubers in one hand and parboiled rice porridge in an earthen bowl in the other. She placed them in front of him and smiled.

"It's a good time," Kodanddi remarked.

Their faces blossomed when they saw Kodanddi. "Come Kodanddiyetta, come," Veluthu said, standing up as a mark of respect.

"Be seated," Veluthu invited him. Kurinchi brought a wooden plank to sit on and water in a bronze water pot to wash his hands and face.

At first, Kodanddi refused their invitation. But on compulsion, he yielded. "I have had my porridge early," Kodanddi said. "I'll just join you."

"It's our good fortune," Veluthu said.

Kurinchi brought roots and porridge. Kodanddi took one root, peeled it and began to munch.

"It's very tasty," he said, looking at her. She smiled beautifully. "Where are your parents?" said Kodanddi.

"Gone to the woods," Veluthu said.

"What for?" Kodanddi asked.

"Digging roots," Kurinchi replied.

He drank a mouthful from the bowl and got up, wishing them a happy family life with all prosperity.

When he rose and was about to leave, Kurinchi said, "How is our Thamburatty?"

"Getting on well," Kodanddi said. "You needn't call her Thamburatty. Just call her '*Edathi*.'" (Elder sister.)

"Oh! Sorry," she said and then asked, "When is the date?"

"Delivery date?" Kodanddi asked with a smile. "It may fall in the next week." He couldn't conceal the happiness of becoming a father.

"Food and drink?" she said.

"As usual," was his response.

"Medicine?"

"Nothing in particular." Then he said, "Now she has totally become one among us." He hastened towards his home, leaving the couple to nibble the taste of honey. It was almost midday, cloudy but extremely hot. It seemed that it would rain in the afternoon. He felt very thirsty and wished for a pot gourd of buttermilk to drink.

On reaching home, he was struck dumb with horror and amazement to see the King's men standing on his verandah carrying swords. They were six of them. Concealing his perplexity, he went straight to them.

"Oh! Bosses, you stand all this time. Can't you sit and rest?" Kodanddi said. He went inside and brought two new mats made of pandanus and laid them out for them.

"We haven't come to sit and chat with you." said one of the King's men in a contemptuous tone; he seemed to be their leader.

"It's my courtesy," said Kodanddi.

"What?" one of them quizzed with anger.

"To honour my guests," he said with humility.

"We haven't come for your reception but to find the princess, Rajalakshmi," said the chief.

"Oh! That's why you have come," remarked Kodanddi calmly.

"Can you help us?" said the chief.

"Oh! Sure," Kodanddi said as calmly as he could. "Please be seated, bosses. Shall I take *Sambaram*[53]?" he invited them.

The chief took his seat, followed by the others on the spread mats. The chief nodded his head and Kodanddi went inside. Vellachi was not to be found in the kitchen. The trio had been frightened to even take a breath and were sitting in Kasthuri's room.

He took a pot gourd full of buttermilk, added salt and flavours to make it tastier, and with a sufficient number of earthen bowls, brought it to the raised bank of his home where the King's men sat.

Drinking the cool tasty buttermilk, they quenched their thirst.

"Now, Kodanddi tell us where is Rajalakshmi, the exiled princess?" the chief said.

"My wife Kasthuri is here. I don't know whether she is a princess or not," Kodanddi said strategically to them.

"Oh! Is she here? Let's see whether she is the princess," said one of the King's men.

"Wait, men, Let me find out," the chief said. The buttermilk

---

[53] Buttermilk.

had cooled their tempers and made them calm.

"You shouldn't put pressure on her. She is in the advanced stage of pregnancy," Kodanddi told them.

"Let's see if it's the princess first," the chief said and got up. All the other King's men got up too. They went inside with Kodanddi. Vellachi and Mali Manikyam got up as soon as the King's men entered and stood to one side.

Rajalakshmi sat upright on a pedestal made of wood, covering her breast and stomach with a mantle.

The chief looked at her, and she looked at his eyes. The chief recognised her the moment their eyes met.

A sudden numbness caught hold of him. He saw the queen sitting on the throne in his inner eye. He bowed his head respectfully and withdrew suddenly. His assistants followed him.

On the raised bank, the chief asked, "How did she happen to be here?"

"She had been abandoned in the woods to die. Smallpox had affected her from head to foot. While I was checking my snares, I heard her groaning. A pathetic groan it was! I went near and identified her as a member of a royal family. I gave her water to drink," said Kodanddi.

"Didn't you enquire where she came from?" the chief asked.

"She was so weak she couldn't utter a word. I thought she would die," Kodanddi said. "Then I left her to die, but on my father's instruction, I returned with millet porridge. She drank two or three leaf ladles of porridge, which evoked my expectations that she might live. We took her home. My mother treated her with food and herbs, and she slowly recovered," Kodanddi said.

"Didn't she wish to return?" the chief asked with an enquiring look on his face.

"She dared not," Kodanddi said abruptly.

"Why?" The chief raised his eyebrows.

"She thought that she wouldn't be safe at the *Kotta*."

"How do you know that?" the chief asked suspiciously. "Either you seduced her or didn't allow her to go," he alleged.

"It would be better for you to ask her." Kodanddi was brave enough to defy them.

Then he went inside and came back with a gun. It was a heavy country-made gun, indeed a flintlock. "Unfettered wild beasts could turn up in the evening," he said while loading it.

The King's men looked at each other. Then the chief called out Mali Manikyam. Taking her aside from the others, he talked to her for some time.

Then the King's men hurriedly quit the hillock. The cool wind began to blow, pushing the abundant dark clouds from west to east. Soon it became very dark, much earlier than sunset.

Back in Kasthuri's room, Vellachi began to quiz Manikyam. "What did the chief say to you?"

"He told me to take good care of her," Manikyam said vaguely.

"That could be said openly," Kasthuri remarked.

"He talked to you secretly," said Vellachi.

"He offered big rewards to me," Manikyam said, not facing them.

Kodanddi smelt impropriety in her answer but didn't say anything. He gestured them not to quiz Manikyam further, for he feared it might adversely affect Kasthuri, yet they had relief for the time being.

Kodanddi began to string together a series of incidents since he found Kasthuri in the woods. At first, it looked like a plot to kill Kasthuri, but plan got thwarted, and for a long time, there had been no query or threat. The searches for her began soon after she visited the herbal physician. He might have reported about her pregnancy to the high place. He thought earlier they cared not whether Kasthuri lived or not. But her pregnancy was keeping the soldiers away. Then it dawned on him that his unborn child was the wanted one.

Fearing that would make them frantic, he didn't share this with Kasthuri or Vellachi. He could share with them at the right time, he thought.

"Those who come may come," he said to himself. "They won't stay away for long."

Manikyam nursed Kasthuri well. Vellachi cooked her favourite foods. The heavy rain and mist kept the tribes confined in their huts. The hillock was shuddered by the thunder while the lightning adorned a necklace of gems to it.

For more than a month, it rained incessantly. The tribesmen feared that their paddy would be washed away.

But at the end of the *Karkkidekam*[54] the sky suddenly brightened itself. There were sudden outbreaks of rain followed by bright sun simultaneously.

All of a sudden, the paddy began to blossom and Kodanddi, and others made arrangements for a night guard.

The slushy green paddy with small white flowers shone on the hill tract. Their dreams, too, shot into spikes along with the paddy. The spikes were dense.

They had made two large tents, one on the Laurus cassia and the other on the Racemose. The two were within shouting distance of each other. Kothumban, Karuthumbu and two others took the responsibility of the night guard happily. Actually, they had their eyes upon uninterrupted feasting and drinking

---

[54] Name of a month in Malayalam era.

throughout the night. Kodanddi glared at them, and they looked down to the ground.

"If you feast up at night, wild boars will make a feast on the paddy," Kodanddi said to them.

"We'll drink only black tea at night," Kothumban promised to guard well.

They returned to the hill tract with lanterns, portable fireplaces and tin sheets. Two country-made guns were also brought for fake gun shoots to keep the wild animals away. For some, drumming on tin sheets wouldn't work.

They kept the firewood in the fireplace all night and hung a light lantern till dawn. Sometimes the lantern would be blown out for want of kerosene or in the heavy wind and rain. But the drumming went on throughout. Sometimes they fired the guns too. The hill tract resembled a folk festival.

When tired from drumming, Kothumban sang,

"Let the black rain clouds roar
Let the sky tear apart widely
Let there appear several youthful women
And I be there alone with them."

Sitting in the Racemose, Karuthumbu, a spontaneous poet, sang,

"Let the beautiful women come with lust
Let their eyes reflect erotic gestures and fragrance
Let their movements be voluptuous
And I be an amorous lover."

Some nights were too vigorous when the duo were intoxicated with hootch. The hillock trembled with the sound of drumming. The hills around reverberated.

Several new men joined the night guard party as hootch and antler's meat were abundant. Karuthumbu's voluptuous jokes cheered them. Night guarding had become neither horrible nor boring but a thrilling duty. Needless to say, it had become ducks and drakes with hootch and meat.

Kodanddi walked to the hill tract morning after morning; sometimes he visited the night guards and chatted with them. He feared the ostentatious guarding might ruin the cause. "Never forget our cause," Kodanddi said.

"We were active the whole night," Kothumban expressed his sincerity.

"I know, but…" Kodanddi stopped halfway, then he said, "People here have no other way to feed their children."

"We know it well. We will take care," Karuthumbu answered.

"That's good. The people have put their trust in you," Kodanddi said. Karuthumbu smiled in gratification.

The drizzling in the morning sun was so beautiful as the water drops dispersed the beams. The glittering water drops adorned the plants as ear studs.

A herd of wild goats darted from the woods and headed towards the hill tract paddy. Kodanddi felt a sudden burning sensation in his stomach. At once, he rushed to the hill tract. He feared that the wild goats would destroy the paddy.

As he ran uphill, he was completely exhausted. The goats had begun their feasting on the spikes. They trampled on the paddy and ran away. His devilish howling mixed with incessant drumming might have frightened them.

He feared they would soon return. The delicious taste of the tender spikes would attract them.

"Guarding must be done during the daytime, too," he said to himself. "Nothing will remain to be reaped otherwise."

As he trumpeted frantically, the tribal men came running, carrying sticks and choppers.

All were grieved to see the trampled paddy. Women agreed to guard during the daytime if dogs were provided. And thereafter, the hillock reverberated with the drumming and barking of the dogs throughout the day and night until the harvesting was done.

Chapter 11

It was the full moon day in the month of *Chingam*. The hillock seemed pleasant and sunny. There were no clouds. The spring had begun. The trees and plants which were stunted in the heavy rain sprouted new shoots.

The bunches of buds and flowers swung in the cool gentle breeze spreading fragrance from the new blossoms.

The trickling rivulets gave tunes to the warbling of cuckoos filling the hillock with an atmosphere of plentiful music.

The peasants were in the hill tract to reap the paddy. The harvest was so rich. Just a single base formed a sheaf of the paddy spikes, which were thick and heavy. Bending low on the spikes, men and women reaped them and tied them to sheaves.

Kothumban carried them to the threshing ground. Some sang folk songs, and others followed.

Kodanddi threshed the sheaves while Kothumban heaped them at a corner. Reaping and threshing went on simultaneously so that by evening the paddy could be carried to their homes.

All the men and women worked tirelessly, forgetting how much their hands and bodies hurt.

As the threshing progressed, the paddy heap bulged minute by minute. The chaffs were too little. Yet they winnowed the paddy before filling their sacks.

Before the sun set, the procession carrying the paddy down the hill tract began.

The pangs of childbirth had begun a long time before

Kodanddi reached home. Vellachi and Mali Manikyam were actively nursing Kasthuri, and Kodanddi waited outside.

The full moon rose to the eastern sky of the hillock, and Kasthuri gave birth to a rising sun in the hut. Manikyam was astonished to see the unique grandeur of the baby. She was waiting for the placenta to be removed, and she demanded a knife to cut the umbilical cord. Kodanddi heard the baby's cry.

Manikyam removed the placenta thrown out of the vagina. She wiped the child with a soft cloth dipped in warm water. Then she cleaned Kasthuri and changed the mat, wiped her with warm water and dressed her in clean clothes. Mother and baby lay aside on a new mat.

"Give her some millet porridge," said Manikyam to Vellachi. Vellachi ran to fetch the porridge.

"It's ready," she said. Vellachi sat beside her, and using a leaf spoon, she poured warm porridge into Kasthuri's mouth. She drank and smiled. Soon the baby began to cry.

"The prince is hungry," said Manikyam.

She squeezed out the nipple of Kasthuri's breast. Then she made her lean towards the child and placed the nipple into the baby's mouth.

To everyone's astonishment, the child began to suck the breast milk. Manikyam called Kodanddi to come inside to see his son, the prince.

He was extremely pleased to see his radiant little son. He gave Manikyam a gold sovereign. Mali Manikyam smiled. She placed it in her hip pocket.

"My duty is over," she said to Kodanddi.

"No, Manikyam, Mom can't do it alone. Kodanddi looked at her while he said it.

The scene of whispering flashed through his mind. He

doubted whether it had any connection with her undue haste. But he didn't share his thoughts or not care tuppence about it.

The baby cried. Kasthuri leaned towards it and inserted her nipple into its mouth. At once, the cry stopped.

"Manikyam, look, you must make her and the baby bathe every day. Mom is old. So...." Kodanddi said.

"So... What?" she said with a feeling of disgust, looking at the ground.

"Stay a few more days," said Kodanddi. "You'll be rewarded."

"I can't stay more than a fortnight," she said with finality.

"We'll have to make *pettulehyam* too." He was looking into the distance while he said it.

"That we can do before I go," she said with a sigh.

"Anyhow she should be delayed from leaving," Kodanddi muttered. He thought of ways to delay her leaving. But at the same time, he thought that she had her own family and would have her own aspirations.

She might report the childbirth to the King's men, Kodanddi feared. The prince must be spared at any cost, he firmly decided.

He couldn't sleep that night, though the much-awaited delivery gave relief to all. While his thoughts ran without bridle, Manikyam and Vellachi nursed the mother and baby.

"It's crucial for two days," Manikyam said. She slowly turned Kasthuri to one side and then the other to check whether there was any bleeding. Having found nothing, she seemed satisfied.

They had a short sleep in the wee hours of the day.

Vellachi had got up early. Perhaps, she hadn't slept. She made parboiled rice porridge and garlic chutney for breakfast.

The thezhuthama[55] condiment was also there as a special side dish.

Manikyam helped Kasthuri to go for toileting behind a bush and made her wash. Then she washed her hands and face. Using a leaf spoon Vellachi made her drink rice porridge. In succession, she gave her garlic chutney and the side dish.

When Kasthuri gestured to stop after a few spoonfuls, Manikyam said, "You have a delivered stomach; you should eat double."

She ate four or five spoonfuls. "It's enough. I can't eat any more." Then she washed her hands and mouth and lay beside the baby. Leaning towards her son, she began to feed him breast milk.

Kodanddi went into the chayippu to visit his wife and son. He saw her happily feeding the prince.

Hearing the footstep, she tried to sit up, freeing the nipple from the baby's's mouth. The prince began to cry.

"No, you give him milk. He's hungry," Kodanddi said with a smile.

"Oh! He's as naughty as you," Kasthuri said, laughing.

Kodanddi sat beside her and caressed her forehead. Leaning low, he kissed on his son's cheek.

Manikyam was out in the open space boiling the *vethu* with medicinal herbs in a large copper cauldron. When boiled for a long time, the essence of the herbs gave it an odour and brown colour.

The odour of the '*Vethu*' sprang into the air. Manikyam put out the fire and allowed it to cool to a bearable warmth.

Then she took the baby and oiled its head and body well. Stretching her legs, she put the new bornon her calf and poured

---

[55] A medicinal shrub used as amaranthus.

the lukewarm '*Vethu*' slowly on its body. The baby didn't cry but smiled. Vellachi stood beside Manikyam for assistance.

It seemed to them that the baby was enjoying the medicinal bath. Having wiped him well, she lay the child on a soft silk mattress. Vellachi sat beside the baby.

Manikyam led Rajalakshmi to the outside bathroom, screened by a rattan mat and made her sit on a wooden log. She oiled her plentiful hair, and body.

"Your hair's like Palmyra bunch," Manikyam said, massaging her abundant breasts, swelled with milk, spacious back and shapely figured loins with '*Kuzhabhu*' she left her to sit for some time on the log. Then she poured the warm *vethu* on her and washed well.

Manikyam wiped her hair and body with a thick bath towel. Dressed in a new double cloth, Kasthuri toddled slowly in. Vellachi served her steaming parboiled rice, added ghee to it and a less spicy condiment. Kneading ghee with hot rice, she ate till her stomach was full.

Hearing the child's cry, she went in to feed him breast milk.

After a short while, the news of childbirth permeated the tribal village. Tribesmen and women with their children came from far and near with gifts to the newborn prince.

Some brought ear studs and anklets, some bracelets and bangles; others rings and dresses. One brought honey and Acorus calamus and another one jar of gooseberry honey. Seeing the radiant prince, all were delighted.

Vellachi and Kodanddi served them food and drink to their satisfaction. The visitors went back with their stomachs and minds filled as well.

For weeks on end, there were visitors. The gifts were piled up. They were moved by the innocent love shown by the peasants. Yet the thoughts mortified Kodanddi's heart as the day of departure of Manikyam drew near.

The days passed by without any untoward or unprecedented happenings. People living on the hillock were happy after the rich harvest. They planted vegetables and hunted edible animals. Wild boars and reddish deers were in plentiful supply. Rarely did they hunt bison and antlers. Hootch and meat were their favourite items.

Some wandered in the woods for wild roots, and others for wild honey. Men and women sold forest produce and hootch to the villagers far and near in the morning and returned in the evening with their purses filled. Arrack and dried stag's meat were sold at a cheap price. Twangulated Gambogio Gardenia was another favourite produce for the villagers.

Men and women bought what they wanted on their return, such as clothes from the '*Saliya*[56] *teruvu*' or earthen pots from the potters or oil from the '*Chakkala*'[57].

Karthumbu would often sing,

"*Panku vettante Enna thechittu thumbalum vali thooralum.*"[58]

When he broke wind, he ridiculed the oil's quality. His sharp tongue spared no one.

Kodanddi had brought everything needed for making *pettulehyam*.[59]

For the next two days, they were engaged in crushing, grinding and pulverizing. Vellachi picked up the *thettamparal*

---

[56] A community of weavers.
[57] The shed where oils are extracted from seeds.
[58] After having used the oil of Mr Panku brother, he has sneezing and farting.
[59] The elixir vital medicine by alchemists to restore health after delivery.

scattered about while crushing. Several tribeswomen helped them to clean and pulverise the medicinal herbs, and the premises were filled with the sweet aroma that penetrated their nostrils.

Vellachi instructed the women one after another.

"Oh! Kurinchikutty, the carom carvi should be powdered finely," Vellachi said to Kurinchi. She was casting her eyes on everything and everyone. Manikyam and two women brought a large flattened round bronze vessel and fixed it on the hearth. Then she poured gingely oil into the vessel and ignited the firewood. When the oil began to boil, Manikyam added the ingredients of the *lehyam* one by one and stirred it with a wooden ladle.

It was a hazardous task, but Manikyam handled it so well. For hours she toiled, making the hazardous work seem easy. The atmosphere was filled with the smell of the *lehyam*. When it was cooled down, the dark brown jelly-like substance was transferred into a large jar made of porcelain. The rest was shared among other women who were so happy to have it.

After the meals, at the chattering hour, Manikyam told them, "My duty is over. I must go." She was casting her eyes at Kodanddi, though in the dim light of the oil lantern, she couldn't see his expression.

"If you say it so suddenly…" Kodanddi didn't complete it. He said, "Of course, we shall try." Then he raised his head and asked, "When are you going?"

"At the earliest," was her reply.

"I'll arrange for day after tomorrow," he said without looking at her.

Four months had passed since she came, and she had been a family member, uncomplaining and adjusting but coquettish.

Two men and two women were arranged to carry the paddy

and other offerings to her home.

Kodanddi gave her gold and silver coins in addition to paddy and other grains. Kasthuri gave her a necklace and Vellachi a nose stud.

Manikyam had gained a good amount of wealth as the delivery was a royal one. But man's greed has no end. Kodanddi couldn't think of her as a culpable wheedler. The thought of whether he had pegged Manikyam in properly began to annoy him at times. Yet he believed in the virtue of man above all.

The effing and blinding she made before leaving put him out of kilter.

Vellachi toiled hard though her age was against straining. She had to make Kasthuri and the baby bathe in the '*Vethu*' and prepare food three times a day.

Kodanddi helped her in washing and cleaning, and yet sometimes she was baffled a lot. She would often say, "Oh! I can't pull it along; I am aged."

"Oh, Mom, We'll engage someone if we are lucky enough to find someone," Kodanddi would say.

"How many times have you said it? It occurs to me like growing breast to the hen," Vellachi said, laughing.

"No, it's not like that, Mom. Kurinchipennu will surely come. But the matter is her paramour would come often," said Kodanddi.

"That doesn't matter. I'll take the broomstick to him."

She wouldn't allow such wantonness. Though Kodanddi never wanted to support adultery, Kurinchi yielded to her master agreeably, only to alleviate her grievances. Kurinchi readily accepted the offer, and she knew that Vellachi was very generous and she could eat and drink sumptuously. And further, she and her lover could enjoy the revelry. The woods and rivulet would be their garden of love.

Kurinchi, neither dark nor fair, had a well-proportioned bodily structure, always had an alluring look, and seemed sexy. The fairly round breasts and beautiful naval were enough to fill lust in the passionate.

"*Thachiye, Vellachi thachiye,*" Kurinchi entered the house, calling.

"Kurinchi, come inside," Vellachi said from the kitchen. She was sweeping.

"*Thachiye*[60]. What shall I do?" Kurinchi said.

"You wash the clothes of the baby in the rivulet," Vellachi instructed her.

Kurinchi found the clothes soaked in urine and faeces of the baby piled up in the corner of the chayippu where the mother and the baby lay. She gathered them and walked towards the rivulet. Several times she covered her nose with the palm of her hand. She felt sick two or three times.

"Excreta is excreta," she said to herself, "whether it's the prince or princess."

It took a long time to wash away the filth and foul smell. Then she immersed the clothes in water made pleasant with the leaves and flowers of Laurus Cassia for fragrance before spreading them to dry in the bright sun.

When dried, the clothes had a sweet smell.

Kasthuri appraised Kurinchi for it. She was grateful for transforming the foul smell into fragrance.

Vellachi fed her sumptuously with steaming rice and elk's meat dish. Kurinchi ate greedily.

Then Kurinchi made arrangements for boiling the *vethu*.

But for making Kasthuri bathe, it was Vellachi's turn. When

---

[60] Grandmother.

Mali Manikyam was there, she looked after everything.

An ostentatious royal bath in medicated water first and then in fragrant water flavoured by the leaves and flowers of the knotty tree.

Kurinchi then swept the rooms and the courtyard, and Vellachi became very pleased with how well she worked.

Then she heard a sharp whistling from the deep woods, unlike the warbling or the falcon but capable enough to penetrate the ears with its shrilling noise. Kurinchi seemed uneasy.

It was her lover's call. But she couldn't meet him. Vellachi had strictly instructed against it. She would only meet him in the evening after the day's work was over.

She feared that if she didn't turn up, he would not be happy. She felt like a civet cat locked up in a cage.

Then she heard a sharp whistle from behind a nearby bush. She couldn't withstand it and ran towards the bush just to inform him that they would meet in the evening, and she came back before Vellachi noticed anything. Having thus adjusted herself, Kurinchi kept working. Vellachi felt at ease and leisurely.

Kodanddi was after an alternative if the King's men came again. Upon the rocky hillock, he sat under an Astonia Scholaris tree which grew spreading on all sides.

Watching from there, he could see the people who were ready to climb the hillock from the foot of the hill from a faraway distance. Just their walking from the foot of the hill to the hillock gave more than sufficient time for him to escape into the dark woods.

But if they arrived unnoticed, they would start bullying him and his family.

"They would come only in the morning," Kodanddi inferred to himself. "They wouldn't be on the hillock at night."

So, morning after morning, he was seated on the rock, watching the foot of the hill. "And further, Manikyam wouldn't betray us." He was looking for the break of the cocoon for a relief.

Days and weeks passed by. Kodanddi hasn't shown any complacency or contention. On a Sunny morning, he saw six or seven men climbing the foothill, and his heart skipped a beat.

He ran home and told Vellachi and Kasthuri about the King's men turning up. There was enough time to escape. Slowly, taking the things they needed, the family went deep into the darker woods sufficiently to hide from the King's men.

Kasthuri found hiding in the woods a little baffling. Kodanddi carried the prince child.

"The child may cry," he said. "So we shall have to move far away so the cry cannot be heard."

Kurinchi didn't understand anything. Yet she followed them, carrying water and food.

Vellachi had caught hold of Kasthuri's hand, anticipating she might slip.

Reaching a small but beautiful waterfall, Kodanddi stopped and said, "It's enough. We'll take rest under the Palmyra."

Velachi took the child and placed him on her lap. Kasthuri sat near. The child looked at their faces simultaneously.

The jingling of the waterfall was a chatterbox to the prince, and the swaying of the Palmyra became an ornamental fan. The flowery thicket with innumerable buds was the canopy to the prince. The prince and the grandmother smiled, showing their toothless gums.

Kasthuri gave breast milk to her son. He drank plentifully and smiled, but not for long as if he knew the seriousness. As the wood was thick and dense, it was semi-dark, with no view of the sky. But the call of hunger reminded them that it was half past noon.

Kurinchi served them food and drink and under the Palmyra they slept. Kurinchi guarded them well.

It was getting dark. The chafers had become active. Kurinchi heard the crowing of the wild cock. She aroused them, and they hurriedly returned home. Vellachi and Kasthuri found it a little difficult to follow Kodanddi, who walked ahead with the prince.

"Why couldn't you call us earlier?" Kodanddi said to Kurinchi.

"I thought you would be annoyed if I woke you," Kurinchi said in her usual nasal tone. It was the day before the new moon day. Of course, there were no stars. No one could see each other's faces.

Somehow they reached home, groping in the darkness.

Vellachi found the lamps and ignited them from the fireplace. To their wonder, nothing had been touched by the King's men. Everything was intact and in order.

"Then why had the King's men come?"

It seemed to be reverberating in their ears, sometimes trumpeting. An illiterate forest dweller couldn't have inferred. But Kasthuri could conjecture an answer.

Chapter 12

Samanthan Chathunni Nayanar sent word to his steward to appear before him with the accounts of the land rent tenancy. Sitting on a swinging cot on the verandah of his Bungalow, he was tallying the amount of money collected and paddy measured with that of the previous year. He was expecting the arrival of his steward.

Soon Kunhikuttan stood in front of him submissively with records of the collection. Nayanar, all of a sudden, got down to the real nitty gritty.

"How is the collection of land rent from the tenants this year?"

"Not up to the expected mark, My Lord," he said. Then he explained, "The measurement of paddy has been increased, but the amount of money collected is less than that of the previous year."

Then he began to read the detailed amounts of the money collected and paddy measured from each Desam[61] date by date. It went on for a long time. Many times, Chathunni Nayanar intervened, and his steward answered all his questions.

"Oh! What a pity! It won't be sufficient to remit in the treasury," exclaimed Nayanar.

"You might convince the King," said the steward.

"How can we get along?" Nayanar was sceptical of going ahead. Then he remarked that the tenants have become impudent.

---

[61] Part of the village.

"Oh! No, they didn't get anything last year from their cultivation. Have mercy on them," Kunhikuttan pleaded. He always had a sympathetic attitude towards them. Being peremptory, Nayanar couldn't bear the indignation.

"One-third of the janmam had been lost to the Mannanar. Four desams and forty thousand acres. What an arrogant decision," Nayanar lamented with a sense of loss.

"It was the King who took the decision; what could we do against it?" Helplessly the steward looked at him. He saw rage building up on the landlord's face.

"But some how it should be ended." The landlord seemed to be firm and belligerent.

"But how? Not only the King but the '*Thukkidi Sayippu*' [62] also backed him." Kunhikuttan, who knew the strength of the Mannanar, said. But it seemed a little toe-curling though trifling to the landlord.

"Let it be so," Nayanar said. "We shall look for other ways." He knit his brows while he said it.

"Other ways!" the steward exclaimed.

"Yeah! Other ways. I'm looking for them," said Nayanar.

"What ways?" The steward's excitement hadn't receded.

"I'll take you into confidence when the time comes."

This shrewdness was alien to the simple-minded steward. "Isn't he a libertine?" the landlord raised his face and said.

"Of course. It seems to me that his lust will never end." Then he went on, "Two or three weeks ago, he abducted a young girl as an eagle snatched a hen, chewed and spat out like sugarcane refuse," he explained. "He never showed the sign of an aphrodisiac."

---

[62] The British District Collector.

"Did the peasants protest?" Nayanar asked. "No one dared," Kunhikuttan said.

"Are the people scared of him?" Again Nayanar was quizzical.

"Absolutely."

"Why were they so much scared?"

"His words are the laws of his desams,"

"So what?"

"Further, he is a master of martial arts," Nayanar grunted and said. "Duel won't do any good." The steward nodded his head as a type of approval of his master. But he said, "There is resentment among the people."

"Can't we fuel it?" Nayanar said, thinking about a way of struggle.

"It'll slowly die out," Kunhikuttan slowly and emotionlessly said in a whispering voice.

"No, we shouldn't allow it to die out," Nayanar frowned. "We should make it spread like wild fire in the mid-summer. The low-bred clumsy Mannanar should be put down," he bawled out angrily.

Hearing the loud human voices, ladies and children came out to the verandah from the inner rooms and listened. He regretted his sudden outflow of emotions.

Having found nothing incongruent, the ladies and children retreated to the bungalow.

Then lowering his voice, he said to his steward, "Think it over at home. How can we execute it? Only we two know about it. Don't let it be known to anybody," Nayanar warned.

Kunhikuttan, who was leaning on a pillar of the Bungalow, went near to the landlord and said, "Mannanar will chop off my head if he comes to know about it."

"Oh! Coward, why are you so worried?" Nayanar said with contempt.

But Kunhikuttan was earnest. He said, "I'm only reminding you of his strength."

"That's good." Nayanar began to listen to his words, so he continued. "It's better to know the strength and weakness of the enemy."

"The good old steward is not trifling," Nayanar said to himself.

"The Mannanar himself is a very good archer. He has eight *kalaries* with hundreds of archers. What will we do if they come together with arms?" The steward couldn't conceal his fear.

"They'll have to sit in the *kalari* [63] with their '*Vayithari*'[64]. We'll look for others."

The landlord still insisted on his other ways, which the steward couldn't make out. And it seemed a mysterious one to him. Perhaps it would be better to keep it as a mystery like so many feudal deeds of the past.

"It's a powder keg with two phases." Nayanar paused for a while as if he was thinking. Then he said, "The first is making the people aware of his wrongdoings." Then he said, "Hasn't he brought ostracism upon women?"

Kunhikuttan took a long squeezy breath, and it seemed to him an uncrackable nut.

Seeing him silent, Nayanar said, "The other is a revolt."

"Nayanar seemed to be virulent towards the Mannanar, But he is prescient," Kunhikuttan said to himself.

"You have relatives there?" said Nayanar.

"Where?"

---

[63] The place where martial arts are practised.
[64] Verbal explanation of the steps made in kalari performance.

"In Mannanar desams?"

"Of course, so many."

"Do you visit them?"

"Occasionally."

"Then you make your visits frequent," suggested Nayanar.

"What can I gain from them?" Kunhikuttan had become timorous.

"Confidence, you get with the programme in Mannanar Desams," proposed Nayanar.

"Me? Me alone?" the frightened steward said.

"No, I'm with you," assured the landlord. It gave some relief to the steward.

The weary lean, grey-bearded steward had been reliable and trustworthy to the landlord since the beginning of his stewardship and had carried out all his commands with sincerity, forgetting his family consisting of his wife and three grown-up girls not yet given in marriage.

"Any how the girls should be sent out," the steward said to himself.

"After that, the Mannanar may chop off my head," he contented to himself.

He slowly retreated towards his home, thinking of the duties he would have to perform.

"The caste Hindus would extend their support but would run away when the actual confrontation takes place. Any how the womaniser should be put an end to," the steward muttered.

"It is a disgrace to all," Nayanar's words rang in his mind. "To be ruled by the son of a prostitute."

He could go to the Mannanar desams curiously searching for bridegrooms without raising suspicion through the lane and midways, talk to the immediate relatives about his grievances, though the Nayanar was making him jump through hoops. *If it were hitting a home run, there would be many,* the steward thought as he reached home.

His mind boggled as he entered the Mannanar desams and, at times, slipped to shoot an arrow against the Mannanar from his disguised journey. Several proposals came to his daughters, of which two or three were suitable.

It made Kunhikuttan more enthusiastic. His frequent visits hit the bull's eye though he was dicing with death.

The resentment against the womaniser grew day by day among the caste Hindus.

The Mannanar, even in his middle age, was still a dandy who kept an avaricious eye on young women.

A libertine, otherwise an able ruler who was skilled in martial art, valourous and invincible, he always walked outside the Kotta escorted and armoured. The jealous aristocrats would take him on if they got a chance. He knew this for certain.

Yet the people saluted Mannanar when they met him or got up in reverence when they happened to see him.

But a broomstick could not sweep off the caste superiority. The ill feeling of being governed by a despicable fellow haunted the caste Hindus. Though the King had anointed the Mannanar and the white people had approved him, the contempt from the high class never alleviated; it mounted day by day. One day the volcano would erupt and make the lava flow down and destroy everything.

Mannanar knew nothing of this sort of anti-movement. Though the majority of the caste Hindus were ready to revolt against him, the *kalaries*, who he trusted much for his rescue, could keep them at large.

Once the *chittari*[65], he had been full to the brim with tenants measuring twelve thousand *paras*[66] of paddy; now it lay vacant and weedy.

Nayanar sent men to make it fit for dwelling. He had told them that his relatives from South Malabar would be coming soon for a fortnight's stay.

Kunhikuttan was summoned to the landlord's Bungalow one early morning. "What's urgent, my lord?" Kunhikuttan said in anxiety.

"You must be ready to go to Sreekunnam at once," Nayanar said, handing over a sealed letter to him.

"What's the matter, Lord? You seem to be in a hurry," Kunhikuttan said nervously.

"Hand this letter to the spice dealer today," Nayanar said.

"Your Lordship didn't disclose the matter," Kunhikuttan said as a humble dependant.

"You do what I said. I'll tell you the matter when you come back." The landlord had a commanding tone.

Kunhikuttan had no other choice but to perform the task.

"Don't let it be known to anybody, Kunhikuttan," Nayanar warned him.

"Your Lordship didn't reveal to me. Then how can I reveal it?" he said.

Nayanar laughed boisterously, which shook his hairy belly. Then he said, "Oh! That I forgot." Kunhikuttan also joined in his laugh.

"I can't trust anyone other than you," he said, looking into the distance.

"So, avoid the conventional path so that nobody can guess

---

[65] An outhouse of the landlord.
[66] A measuring vessel measures 10 kgs of paddy.

your destination."

Kunhikuttan, forgetting his age and fatigue, galloped as swiftly as an arrow. He ignored the hard stones and sharp thorns that pierced his feet.

Food and drink or something of those sorts were secondary to him. After performing his task, on his return, he would visit the toddy tapper, Birundan, gulp two bottles of pure coconut toddy with fish molly and would walk home frolicsomely.

Apart from toddy tapping, Birundan fished from the river. His wife cooked the fish savoury and tempting. The very remembrance would enable a plentiful flow of saliva into the customer's mouth.

The spices dealer was in the *Pandikasala*[67] adjacent to the spices market. The conviviality he showed was remarkable and betrayed the presentiment.

Kunhikuttan handed the letter to him, which he opened and read with utmost care and attention.

Having read the letter, he raised his head and looked at Kunhikuttan, a special kind of look that might have pierced his heart. Then he said, "Tell your lord it shall be done, but you will have to wait."

"What?" the perplexed steward said. "Why will I have to wait?"

The dealer thought that the steward was either ignorant or playing possum. But he said, "They are not here now. When they come, I'll send word to your lordship."

"Who?" said Kunhikuttan. "I don't understand."

The spices dealer thought for a while. "To reveal at this juncture might be dangerous," he said to himself.

"Didn't your lordship tell you?" the dealer said to the

---

[67] The storage house for hill produce.

embarrassed steward. He raised his eyebrows in suspicion.

"No, but he has told me that he would disclose his mind on my return," Kunhikuttan said.

"Tell your lord that I'll inform him on their return," the spice dealer assured him, handing over a letter to Kunhikuttan.

Kunhikuttan began to plod back home, the way dreary, and his mind dissipated. The secret deal was going to be serious but seemed vague to Kunhikuttan. He strolled to Birundan's hut as he knew there wasn't much time left for revelry.

The tapper received the steward with complacency and treated him with unadulterated toddy and food stuffs such as peppered river fish and rice cake. There was no one other than him; the customers were yet to come. He ate and drank sumptuously.

He took out a silver coin from his purse. But Birundan refused to accept the money saying, "What an inglorious man I'll be if I accept money from you." Kunhikuttan trotted back, belching, followed by intermittent farting.

"Ah! Flatulence," Kunhikuttan said to himself.

"I mightn't drink toddy when the stomach is empty."

As he advanced, his vitality mounted high. His movements became swifter and swifter, but he seemed to lose his footing. He feared that he might fall, but could not stop and rest. Kunhikuttan reached home before nightfall.

In the wee hours of the next day, Kunhikuttan reported the matters of the visit to the landlord.

"What unevenness made you so queer yesterday," Nayanar said. He had sheer compunction about his look.

"The spices dealer was in the *pandikasala*. I had to wait for a long time. He promised to carry out your orders as soon as they came," the docile steward said. "He has sent a letter to you." He handed over the sealed letter to the landlord.

The indignation towards his minion ran out of steam to some extent.

"I was on tenterhooks last night since I couldn't see you. We must be on the lookout till we are informed," the landlord said.

He went very near to his steward and began to whisper in his ears about his plan to crush the Mannanar. He was very keen not to let it be known to anybody until the plan's execution.

The whispering went on for a long time, Kunhikuttan raising his concerns and doubts and Nayanar clearing them.

Two weeks later, the spices dealer sent word to the landlord in the affirmative, and the handymen from the south set out in small boats from *Sreekunnam* in the middle of the night and reached *Chittari* during the wee hours of the day.

Everything, foodstuff and drinks, munchies and mats to take rest, were arranged inside the *Chittari*. They didn't have to go out except for going to the toilet. They would take rest during the day time or discuss the modus operandi in detail and strike the target at night.

At daybreak, they saw the lofty Mannanar Kotta without a roof. The devilish figure of the Kotta remained in the morning, fuming with the burnt and naked walls. Its grotesque appearance intimidated the villagers.

How many were killed or how many quit remained a mystery to them. The fumes and charring smell were intense.

Fortune hunters came seeking gold and silver. Some had small fortunes. They forced open the walls, raised platforms for treasures thinking that they might have been dug in the ground or on the walls, and desecreted the Kotta.

The jubilant high class went to public places to express their hegemonic discourses. They had a thousand tongues to speak out against the libertine loftiness of the Mannanar. But there were many who lamented upon his drastic murder, especially the poor and the downtrodden.

Why the hundred or more *kalari archer* kept away from the Kotta on that fateful day became a subject of talk for a long time and remained unknown.

Chathunni Nayanar was overjoyed but bore dreadful anxiety over the consequences. "People may put the blame on the rioters," he said to Kunhikuttan.

"So, we are safe." Kunhikuttan smiled.

"*Thukkidi Sayippu* may send his men for an enquiry," Nayanar expressed his anxiety.

"Let him come and enquire. People will give statements. We needn't bother," the steward consoled his lord.

"Has anyone noticed the henchmen in the *chittari*?"

The valour of the landlord seemed to be evaporated. In fact, he hadn't expected such a terrific attack from them.

"No, nobody came on the way," Kunhikuttan said. "Don't sweat the small stuff," he advised his master. "If so, no need to fear."

Nayanar took a deep breath as if in relief.

"My Jenmam on four desams and forty thousand acres would be retrieved," he said.

Chapter 13

Power was an intoxicant to Vasundhara. The more she tasted it, the greedier she became. Nothing could satisfy her greed like the waves in the sea never ceased.

The King lay on his death bed, timorous though consanguineous never affected her lust. She wanted to sip power elixir to the very last drop. But she never wanted to pick up the gauntlet or bear the dissent.

The moment she knew from Mali Manikyam that a baby prince was born to Rajalakshmi, her rage flamed vigourously as if to consume her.

Like the eagle flying round and round over the landscape to detect its prey and landing suddenly to clasp it between its claws and flying up in the sky, the baby prince should be seized, Vasundhara thought.

"Let a hundred eagles fly over the hillock," she said to herself.

She called out her commandant and ordered him to present the baby prince either alive or dead without delay.

Entrusting ruthless armoured men to the task the commandant proved his loyalty towards Vasundhara, the acting queen.

They were five in number, excelling each other in their cruelty. Setting out very early, they reached the hillock the following day at noon. Having a more powerful eye than the eagles, Kodanddi could notice the landing of the eagles from afar, reaching out to mother nature's lap with the baby prince and others as the little ones under the mother hen's wings

But on that fateful day, the warriors didn't return. They had decided on the fate of the baby prince.

"He's a wild fowl that can't he snared in easily," one of the warriors said. "He has spies, too," said another.

"They keep informing him about our movements," said the third.

"I don't think so. He's only a forest dweller," said the fourth one.

"Then how could he hide each time?" the captain asked.

"Animals act as his spies. They can give signals," the first one said.

"Some birds, too," the second warrior added.

"Let's hide somewhere in the woods and attack, waiting in ambush," said the third warrior.

"Kodanddi knows every nook and corner of the woods. It'd be difficult to face him there," the fourth one expressed his fear.

"What would we do then?" The captain was in a fix.

"Ignite the hut at night. Shoot the residents when they come out," said the first one.

"It's a good idea." the captain said, appreciating the warrior.

"But it's inhuman," said the fourth one.

"What's human in the woods?" The captain seemed to be furious. "Human is not the justice in the woods. It is might," he shouted.

"Who do you want? Kodanddi? Or the princess's child?" The fourth soldier was not to be put down easily by the captain's outburst.

"We want both," said the captain.

"Let's put up at one of the huts tonight and pounce upon his hut earlier than the crowing of the cock," the first warrior put forward his idea.

"That's good," said the captain.

"But Kodanddi is ambidextrous, you know," the fourth warrior said, causing much annoyance to the captain.

"Has your virility been lost on climbing the hillock?" the captain said, looking at him furiously. "But he cannot be silenced easily."

"Can't we wheedle one of his tribe? Giving gold or silver as a bribe? Why can't we put the squeeze on him to abduct the baby prince?" he said, looking at the ground.

The idea seemed too good for them who were suspicious of his bad temper.

There stood a hut aloof from other huts at a walkable distance, an ideal place for the warriors to put up unnoticed.

"Let's go there and get acquainted with them," said the captain. Pokkudan and Kamachi lived in that little hut with their two small children. "Hoi, is there anyone here?" the captain said, entering the courtyard.

"Ah! We are here." Pokkudan came out carrying his little son.

Seeing fire armoured warriors, he was embarrassed. His elder son was toddling on the verandah of his hut and screamed; the younger one followed.

Spreading the grass mat on the raised platform, Pokkudan said, "Oh! You came to my little hut. I'm blessed; please be seated."

The warriors sat on the mat. Pokkudan went inside to hand over the child to his wife. The elder son had already retreated to her back.

"Ah! *Thamburan* didn't say anything." Pokkudan was polite

and subservient. The captain called him aside and whispered in his ears for a long time.

Looking through the crude curtain, others could see the dark shapely Kamachi inside.

"Though dark, she's charming," one of the warriors muttered.

"Indeed a dark beauty," another said somewhat louder, forgetting the situation.

"Hsh… hsh…" the third one warned them.

"You have forgotten why you have come."

"No, I do remember," he said, but he had an apathy on his face that he tried to conceal.

"Alluring another man's wife is sin," he said as if in soliloquy.

"What sort of stuff are you made of? Of wood? Of soil? You seem to be averse to these matters," the second warrior seemed more emotionally human.

"Enough of this nonsense," said the fourth one. The admonished warriors kept quiet in subservience.

In the meantime, the captain and Pokkudan had come to a pact. The warriors saw the captain handing over the sovereigns to Pokkudan, which he pocketed. The captain also offered a small fortune from the queen to Pokkudan for keeping the secret.

Back on the verandah, the captain said to the fourth warrior, "Your suggestion is approved. Let's wait for the crowing of the cock." He strutted forward in recognition.

"You are dexterous, like a fox," the first warrior said to the fourth, appreciating his keen intelligence.

Thrusting his chest forward, he said, "Are you still mocking me?"

"Your supper?" Pokkudan said submissively.

"No need for you to worry. We have brought something," said the captain.

They discussed their plans, lowering their voices. Yet Pokkudan complained of the loudness. He feared that others would notice. He was worried he would be found out. "Too much noise will alert the people," he said.

They waited for their opportunity. An air of unprecedented calmness prevailed over them. Slowly the sun finished its burning leaving the remnants on the western horizon. The dark hillock yearned to touch the red blaze.

The woods became active with the humming of the cicadas, the grunting of the owls and the howling of the night fowls. The flapping of wings and cooing of bats filled the atmosphere with terror. The self-acclaimed valour and war-mongering of the warriors began to drain little by little.

The cold wind began to blow, making the leaves rustle and the warriors uncomfortable, as the night advanced slowly.

Pokkudan could neither sleep nor sit. He walked in and out of his murky hut. His wife and children had already gone to bed.

But he saw his wife's eyes open widely. She couldn't sleep thinking of his culpable complacency.

The guilt made him restless, and he became a bundle of nerves. Torches were made ready using reeds and cloth pieces soaked in oil.

The night was lengthy and dull. The forlorn cold wind and deafening cicadas kept them awake. Halfway through the night, all the six set out, igniting the torches. It was much before the crowing of the cock.

Pokkudan had become namby-pamby during the restless and starred night. The sleepless night had turned his mind cloudy. But his mentor went on putting the squeeze on him. Half-heartedly he stalked into the house, cutting off the crude curtain at the back of the kitchen.

In the torchlight, he saw Kodanddi sleeping soundly, snoring and wouldn't wake even if the chilliness of the bathing ghat was thrown over him, but Vellachi, a light sleeper, might awake. Pokkudan feared as he was walking stealthily like a cat.

In the next room, he saw the radiant baby prince sleeping beside Kasthuri, inclined towards the left; and she had placed her right hand on the child. He waited for a while. If he took her hand off, she might awake, which would upset everything.

The oil in the torch was on the point of extinction. He couldn't wait any longer. Slowly he took her hand off the child. A royal golden hand it was, warm and smooth. For a moment, he was at a loss. But he was afraid. Pokkudan took the baby prince on his right shoulder and held the torch with his left hand.

Somehow the baby prince knocked the torch, and the hot oil drops spilled on the sleeping baby's right calf; and the baby screamed aloud.

Anticipating the danger, Pokkudan hastened towards the kitchen door and fell on Vellachi, who screamed so loudly she aroused the whole house, including Kodanddi. Not seeing the child beside her, Kasthuri, too, got up screaming.

In the meantime, Pokkudan had managed to dart out. The torch had been blown out, and he groped his way out in the dark with the child still sobbing on his shoulder. He somehow reached the warriors waiting for him, handed over the child to the captain and within no time disappeared into the woods as if he knew Kodanddi was after him with arms. The captain thought it would be risky to be there with the screaming child and decided to eliminate the prince child at once. He raised the prince with his left hand and pulled the sword from its sheath with his right. The baby prince, beaming a radiant smile, glanced at the captain and stunned him for a moment.

So clearly in the torchlight, Kodanddi saw the captain from a distance, holding the baby prince in his left hand and pulling out the sword with sharp glittering edges in his right hand. A dreadful sight it was! But for Kodanddi, there remained no time to lose. Seeing the captain going to chop off the prince's head, Kodanddi couldn't think of anything other than shooting an arrow at the captain's neck.

Drawing the string of his bow beyond his right ear, he shot an arrow into the captain's neck, piercing his trachea. At once, he fell down with the baby prince. Kodanddi shot two more arrows which killed two more. The other two fled from the spot with their lives. Torches had been blown out; only the dim light of the dawn prevailed.

Kodanddi ran to the spot, took the baby prince in his hands and examined him thoroughly, and found that he wasn't harmed. The child was beaming his innocent smile at him.

Then he looked around. Three men lay there with their necks split open, and the blood oozing through the cleft the arrows had made. A pool of blood was forming by itself by the confluence of thin streams.

Kodanddi walked home quickly with the baby prince on one shoulder and the heavy bow on the other. The consequences had not dawned upon him then. The Zealous heroism of having saved the baby prince frothed effervescence to the brim in him.

On seeing him with the prince, Kasthuri and Vellachi came, running and screaming. They went in with the child.

Vellachi wiped the child with a bath towel dipped in warm water and made atonement for the avoidance of fear and to drive away the evil spirits. The salt crystals put in the fire burst out in low sounds, shattering, marking it symbolically.

"The henchmen were trying to kidnap my child," Kodanddi said.

Noticing the blown-out torch, Vellachi exclaimed, "Ah... Ah... Torch. They had come with a torch, see."

"They would have killed my son," Kasthuri said, sobbing.

Kodanddi didn't describe the scene he had witnessed, the captain holding the ankles of the baby prince together in his left hand and the unsheathed sword in his right hand.

On remembering it, he shuddered. What made him so courageous at that time was still unbelievable even to himself, but he thought it had made him equal to the situation.

But soon, a real fear began to hurt him. He had killed three of the King's men, and the acting queen would know for certain who had done it. The men who escaped would report it to her within two or three days, and more soldiers would come for retaliation. His thoughts went on as the sun slowly crept into the sky.

Kodanddi went in and sat beside his wife. Their son was enjoying uninterrupted sleep. Vellachi had begun her work in the kitchen much earlier than usual.

"We'll have to leave this place, my dear," he said to Kasthuri. She raised her eyebrows as if to ask, "Why?"

"You know, of course, you know," he said.

"Oh, yes, I know our son is not safe here." She began to sob.

He wiped her tears with his hands and said, "You shouldn't weep. You're a princess and your son a prince. A prince never wants to see his parents weep."

Kasthuri looked at him in surprise.

"I retrieved our son from the soldiers, killing them."

Her queenly prowess rose high. She said, "You killed?"

"Yeah! Not one but three."

How much pride it gave her was beyond words. "You are a great warrior. I'm proud of you." Kodanddi held his head high with pride.

"We'll have to go far soon. Within two or three days, the army men will come in multitudes," Kodanddi said as he thought about a refuge.

Then he went into the kitchen and told his mother everything that had happened. She goggled at him unbelievingly; then, quiescent for some time sat on a wooden plank with her head supported on an elbow.

The news flashed out in the morning when the people came out of their huts for their routine duties.

The whole of the hillock was there in no time. But most of them retreated to their houses, fearing the consequences. The military would sift the whole of the hillock for the culprits, they said to each other.

Pokkudan was silent. His wife, Kamachi, had warned him against being outspoken.

Two soldiers had fled from the scene, and they knew the truth. But they wouldn't turn up again for fear of losing their heads. Pokkudan was in a conciliatory mode.

In the evening, Kothumban visited Kodanddi and discussed the seriousness of the matter and their plans.

He was amazed to hear about his encounter with the warriors. Kodanddi told him to remove all the movable possessions from his house as soon as he left. The people couldn't leave the corpses as they were not to cremate their bodies, as the authorities should come and prepare the Mahasar before the cremation.

They were waiting for the officials to come. They agreed to provide night guard as well; otherwise, wolves and vultures would feast on the corpses.

The truth couldn't be concealed forever. Yet too many stories roamed about, and the tribes fabricated many of their own.

Some said that the fairies living in the Alstonia scholaris, which stood on the rock, had come down to suck the lifeblood of the soldiers in the middle of the night.

But why the soldiers had come at night couldn't be explained.

Some put the blame on the ferocious animals in the woods who would rarely come out to take human blood. But no one had seen such ferocious animals in their lives. They made the excuse that they wouldn't have been there if they had come across such animals.

And a few said that since it happened on a new moon at midnight, it was the deed of the evil spirits who took revenge on the warriors for their wrongdoings. Why the evil spirits spared the two was out of their perception.

Kodanddi quit the mountain peak in the wee hours of the day along with his mother and wife. Vellachi carried the baby prince, Kasthuri some clothes and Kodanddi the rucksack. He hadn't revealed their destination nor met anyone on the way.

Vellachi sobbed in pain as she stepped down the hillock. She had been there for decades, since her marriage. Her husband and son had given her no suffering but undefinable happiness. Farming and hunting gave them plentiful life. The rivulets gave them cool pure water in almost all the seasons of the year, and the weather used to be fine and encouraging. She would have liked to be there till her death.

Keeping everything in mind, Kodanddi walked ahead with the heavy rucksack on his shoulders and firm footsteps. Vellachi and Kasthuri followed him.

Chapter 14

The mountain peak, in all its evening elegance, held its head high. The red blaze of the setting sun gave the peak a halo of reddish gold.

Kodanddi's family reached the tribal kingdom of *Udaya konon*, *after* daring the ups and downs through the dark and deep woods. They felt pounded and squeezed after the long day's walk.

The tribes received them respectfully and took them to their King, of course, without a crown or a throne. But he always carried a sceptre and looked like the chieftain of a hill tribe.

Kodanddi bowed in front of the King. He took three betel leaves and three Areca nuts in a plantain leaf along with a gold sovereign and placed the plantain leaf in front of him.

He pleaded for a suitable dwelling plot and the right of cultivation and hunting, which the King sanctioned readily.

A *Bhairavi temple* made of dark laterite and four or five small thatched houses roofed with dried grass stood against the pooh-pooh sound of the cold western wind on the top of the peak.

It was their time of worship. The tribes came in scores to have a '*Darshan*' of '*Chamundi*'.

They prayed and offered silver and copper coins to the goddess and got saffron and flowers as '*Prasadams*'.

Kodanddi's family, attended by guards, was sent to the eastern side of the peak, where a hut with bare minimum facilities remained vacant for them to stay in until other arrangements were made. A rivulet with plentiful cool crystal clear water flowed down and was a great solace to them.

At the same time, it posed a high risk of flooding when there was heavy rain. Again there was the threat of wild beasts which would often turn up to quench their thirst. Vellachi made the hearth and ignited firewood, made par-boiled rice porridge and condiments. Dried elk meat fry was also made. After a day-long walk, they were all tired and exhausted. A bath in the rivulet and a meal of steaming rice porridge cast away their tiredness and exhaustion. Soon they fell asleep.

Kasthuri groaned, for she felt her body pounded while others snored. There were tribal men on the mountain's eastern slope in small huts. They were believed to be the descendants of a prime tribe from the North.

Over the centuries, they had been transformed into an indigenous tribe. They spoke, ate and dressed the same. They cultivated on the plains and hunted in the woods. Smithies and weavers were among them. Potters made pots and smithies, ornaments and arms. Weavers weaved clothes.

Kodanddi became one among them as the days passed by. In all the activities, he participated with them, whether it was cultivation or hunting or whatever it might be. But he didn't want to be a noted hero. He feared it would pave the way for unwanted discussion, and living incognito would become impossible.

Vellachi would often say, "Unless you stood up, men wouldn't know whether you were crippled or hunch-backed."

Kodanddi remembered. Yet some had a suspicious eye upon Kasthuri and her son, which he ignored carefully.

Udaya konon had a military, a special kind, for the protection of the tribe. Men not too aged or sick were obliged to serve without payments.

In the afternoon, after the day's work, they must assemble on the mountain peak in front of the *Bhairavy* temple. Men practised bow and arrow, sword, shield and spear.

Kodanddi joined them. But never took the initiative nor performed his heroic deeds. He often talked to them.

He learned that their ancestors were hill tribes who fought for *Kanishka* in the North.

But the rise of *Salivahana* discomfited them, scattered *Kanishka's* forces to smithereens. One such tribe fled to the south. Many times the bickering disintegrated them during their fleeing. Too many lost their lives due to lack of food and water. Drought and flood alike had affected them badly. A small portion of the tribes immigrated to western Ghats and settled on the *Udaya* mountain, and became known as '*Udaya konon*'.

Years passed by. Too much water flowed down from the mountain through the rivulets. Rain, mist and summer cycled around.

The teething troubles of the prince were over. Kodanddi gave initial lessons of martial arts to him. Young Kodanddi mastered them easily as if he had been born for it. Within a few years he became proficient both in fencing and archery. Hunting made him the foremost archer, he could even interlocate a speeding wild goat.

At times father and son practised duel in the remote plains of Udayakonon with the intention of hiding their lights under the bushel. Vellachi and Kasthuri would watch them curiously. Using sticks, they practised fencing if they were not engaged in farming or hunting.

Since there were no horses with the tribes horse riding was not possible for them. Kasthuri had begun teaching alphabet even before Aditya attained five years; at first on sand spread on the ground, later switched on to palmyra leaf and style. But no books were available either of paper or palmyra leaf, and depended much on memory and oral communication.

However she could teach him much of the Vedas and Upanishads which she remembered. Stories from the epics and Panchathantra taught Aditya, the lessons of Rajadharma, and political science from Kautilya's Arthasasthra.

While she delivered the lessons they were teacher and pupil.

Aditya listened to her attentively and often raised queries. How koutilya agglomerated money for the treasury was a subject of wider discussion.

"Koutilya had levied one by sixth of the production of the people."

Kasthuri said

"Is it applicable now a days?" Aditya queried.

"Why not? It would be relevant as long as the world lasts," she said.

"How?" He raised his eyebrows. He had come to the point.

"By its fairness and populace."

Kasthuri explained to him.

"It avoided heavy taxations." She further said.

Aditya Devan felt proud of his mother. Vellachi and Kodanddi were left in the dark. For them it seemed to be a hard nut to crack.

"Do you know how Kautilya charmed the kings?"

Kasthuri asked her son.

He shook his head as a mark of ignorance.

"Kautilya sent glamorous young women to kings far and near to charm them." Kasthuri explained smiling . She was ogling Kodanddi while she said it.

"Staying in the places they would charm Kings and make them allies." She said.

"Then," Aditya said

"They would come back with gifts to the king."

"But there were breaches and hissings, sometimes." Aditya pointed out.

To make the friendship strong and permanent they proposed marriages." She said.

"Then?" Aditya said looking at her.

"We exported spices and so many things won over."

"Then?" Again he asked.

"Money flowed in." she said.

Aditya Devan assimilated all those lessons but had deficiency in mingling with the people.

"Meet them, What otherwise can we do?" Kodanddi suggested.

The season being fine and they were at their leisure, Kodanddi family decided to set out as parivrajakas ebbing at the sea of humanity. Together they trotted down from village to village putting up their nights wherever they reached and eating whatever the villagers gave them.

The peasants received them with food and drink and made provisions for their stay for night with great hospitality. But Kodanddi family didn't reveal their identity. People thought that they were recluses on their pilgrimage, gave them fruits and milk at night.

Men and women were at their work in a paddy field when they reached a village all drenched in the mire, some were carrying cow dung in rattan baskets, leaky through the holes, trickling down their faces. Some were carrying sheafs of young paddy for transplantation. Women were planting young paddy in the muddy water up to their ankles.

They saw women rotating the spinning wheels and men weaving at their looms in a weavers village. Those sights were new to them. Aditya was enthusiastic. His boyish fascinations were towards the thread balls in multi colours. But the dust and dye made Vellachi uneasy and she felt suffocation.

Pottery was another subject of his attraction. Aditya was astonished to see how the clay was transformed to beautiful work of art. He noted the importance of the wheel at the potter too.

"When the wheel is rotated a small block of clay is turned into a vessel!" Aditya exclaimed.

It was to be harnessed and dried before baking," said Kodanddi.

Kodanddi family was at a pottery furnace when he was working at the furnace. It was a large one. Hundreds of pot vessels were arranged into a big heap on a layer of firewood formed into a small mountain of earthen vessels. It was fully covered with hay and firewood. Igniting at night it suddenly became a hill of fire burning all through the night and the following day.

When the furnace was opened on the third day, the potter was shocked to see that there was not even a single vessel remained unbroken.

He lamented upon his loss of several weeks of hard work and fainted. Kodanddi felt pity on him.

But it taught the lesson that all works mightn't yield expected results.

"Life is uncertain as the potter's furnace." The folk people had said.

"Hammering a red-hot iron rod changes its shape."

Aditya noted down while they visited a farrier's workshop. But the smoke and heat in the shed posed a serious problem to them.

For months on end they trotted down through the villages, but had to return before the commencement of monsoon. They returned to Udayakonon before the rain started, but was shuddered to see the forces surrounding it. Vasundhara had deployed forces in the Udayakonon.

Vasundhara sent spies to find the whereabouts of Rajalakshmi and the prince. The spies gathered information from the pilgrims returning from *Nooranad*, a forest town celebrating the *Erumad Makkam Uroos* that a tribal kingdom had been set up on the western Ghats named *Udaya konon*. Kodanddi might have fled to *Udaya konon* with his family and sought asylum. Though apparently there was no threat from the *Udaya konon* to the *Kovilakam*, she feared that external forces may make use of the tribes in the woodlands.

It was difficult for them to put the tribal army down in the woods or shatter them. The disgrace of losing three soldiers, including the captain, on the hillock in the encounter with Kodanddi could not easily be forgotten, but at times it irritated her.

Her uncle, the bed-ridden King, showed no sign of improvement or deterioration in his health. Vasundhara managed the affairs of the state in pomp and splendour. But her ambition for a baby prince before the King's demise remained unfulfilled.

Yet she discussed the encroachment of *Udaya Konon* with her minister and commandant and planned for a woods war in the summer itself to avoid the risky movement of the troops in the rains. The soil would be slippery, and the woods would be full of leeches and reptiles that would stall their advancement, in addition to the camping hazard.

The minister was of the opinion that the Suzerainty of the *Kovilakam* would be approved by the tribal King. They could guard the kingdom on the eastern side if they were taken into confidence. On the other hand, if they were driven away, they would only become waifs and strays.

"Anyhow, we will have to win them over," she ascertained.

"It would be a twin success," said the minister, revealing his statesmanship.

She knew his words were double-edged.

"You mean the victory over the tribe and Rajalakshmi," she said.

"Yeah! Your majesty," he said politely.

The red blaze of the setting sun gave the mountain peak a halo. There sat two glorious figures brilliantly on a rock shaped like the skull of a tusker, the background scene being the reddish gold horizon.

While inspecting, Captain Nambiar and his cops noticed the splendour, a magnificent and rare sight.

The captain and his cops went near. A young sage with unearthly radiance, sat with an old lady equally radiant, not of the tribal type, but seemed to be members of a royal family.

The youth, with his shapely figure, golden complexioned and abundant curly black hair being tied to the top of his head, wore a chain of red *rudraksha* around his neck and seemed a young ascetic who had suddenly turned up from the invisible world. The lady seemed to be his mother or elder sister from their resemblance.

An undefinable peace was on their faces.

At a glance, captain Nambiar was convinced that the saintly

youth possessed splendour not of the ordinary traits of Kshatriya blood was blended together harmoniously.

The captain went near and greeted them. He said, "I'm so fortunate to see you."

Rajalakshmi recognised him. More than seventeen years had passed by. Yet he remembered her.

"You still remember me!" she exclaimed.

"How can I forget you?" The captain said.

The lustre on her face diminished, and two teardrops trickled down her cheeks. She might have remembered her childhood. "You were our hope. Our future," said the captain looking to the ground. He couldn't face her.

"Oh! What a fool I am," he exclaimed. "I didn't ask his lordship's name."

"He's Aditya Devan, my son," Rajalakshmi said, and there was a sense of pride in her voice. They noticed her face blossomed with joy when she said it.

"This prince is the heir of the kingdom," the captain said to his cops. They bowed their heads in respect. They took leave of them. "you should not reveal it to anybody," captain Nambiar said to his cops. "I'll report to the King confidentially and get his consent to bring Rajalakshmi and her son back to the palace. Only after that should anyone know," the captain explained to his fellow men.

Chapter 15

"Oh! My child… My Cuckoo… Don't go, my Dear… please lend me your ears… please… My cuckoo," the King called out at the top of his voice.

His attendants came running and saw him struggling, sweating all over his body. They made him drink water and fanned him. He groaned and grumbled as if in a flurry, making unusual sounds of death throes.

Although the King couldn't rise, he was trying to turn about and was gesturing as if in severe mental agitation. His attendants and security men, not knowing what to do, ran here and there and informed Vasundhara, the acting queen.

Vasundhara trotted towards the Harem, chuntering and disgruntled, and saw her uncle struggling for life, uttering incoherent words as though he was nearing death. She thought that his fateful day has come and she needn't do anything more. The power being inducted in her and the top brass at her feet, though nothing to be feared about, She had never stopped sleuthing on the key men in power, not exempting the lain King. It had never come to her perception that he would get such a long life, and hadn't done any scathing but had made speeches, honey trickling and excessively praising him to win him over. Snooping closely and through her hocus-pocus, she could grasp the nettle.

But someone asked her how it could be that she could retain the power, which made her frantic, though she could rule unless and until there emerged a male descendant; otherwise, she should either give birth to a prince child or hold the coronation ceremony. The time was slipping from her fingers, she thought with self-contempt. The latter would be better if the King would become better.

Nobody could criticise her if things went well; otherwise she would take a beating that would seriously annoy the King. She couldn't evade him as she had done with Rajalakshmi for fear of the people's wrath, for she knew that the people loved him for his endeavour to provide them with a better life. Such heinous thoughts lodged in her when her uncle battled for his life.

For the time being, Vasundhara thought that it was necessary for the King to live on, and sent word to the court physician, who came running, wasting no time, and reverentially examined His Highness's Royal body, thumping on his chest and looking keenly in his eyes and at his tongue but found no pestilent disease.

"His Highness's physique is somewhat better than earlier. Nothing to worry about," the physician said to those who had gathered, giving some relief to them.

"Then why is His Highness throwing himself around so?" said Vasundhara to the physician.

"Something might be worrying His Highness," the physician said.

"What might it be?" said Vasundhara.

"Let's know from his Highness's words," said the physician. But the King had slipped into a nap.

"Now he's sleeping. Let's wait," The obsequious physician said.

Vasundhara and others left, leaving the physician and the two henchmen along with the sleeping King. Waiting patiently, they sat at the office of the chamberlain for the King to wake up.

Hours later, the King woke up. His henchmen made him do his ablutions, bathe in the warm Vethu, apply scents and dress in fresh clothes. When everything was ready, he was made to sit on an inclined bed. Then they made him gulp milk porridge. He swallowed only four or five spoonfuls lying in a resting position.

The physician was called in. Bowing his head, he greeted the King. "What's the problem, your Majesty?" The physician asked politely.

The King was trying to say something. But words wouldn't come out.

"Your Highness has been blabbering all night?" the physician said submissively.

"I don't remember." Somehow the words struggled out.

"Something haunts your noble mind. Try to recollect them, my Lord," the physician said with the utmost respect.

The King stared at him but didn't say anything. It seemed to them that he was bringing forth thoughts from the depth of his mind. The physician waited for his response.

After a long time, he said, "People heard your highness's deliriums last night." Getting no response, the physician continued to persuade the King.

"Your Majesty didn't get sound sleep last night. What's pricking at your royal heart?"

The King, lolling on his inclined bed, mumbled, "Anything for sound sleep?"

"Oh! Yes, my Lord," said the physician submissively. Then he implored, "Let me know what's haunting your Lordship."

The King began stammering out about his overnight hunting. "I was after a bison, a large, fierce and precarious animal in the thick dark woods on horseback. The hooked horns of the bison had arched to form into an elevated or protruded circle whose deadly knocking would severely hurt any mortal who came by. I had shot two or three arrows at the animal, and though they pierced deep into its flesh, it didn't take it seriously. Once or twice, it turned back fiercely; its nostrils were expanded so wide that it seemed to inhale me and frighten me, but my horse wobbled about from the bison's knocking, the heavy hoofs squeezing the earth, in addition to the kicking of the ground created a terrific atmosphere in the woods.

"The birds flew away in fear wailing, the reptiles crawled to their burrows, and I was alone at a faraway distance. My fellow hunters were at the other side of the mountain, must have been searching for me in the mountain pass. Let them search for me. I was not at all scared.

"A new virility was filling me vigorously, and I felt a budding youthfulness, enabling me to fight even with the most ferocious animal. At the same time, I watched the conspicuous animal stride for stride. It seemed invisible, often hectoring me with a presentiment. My conscience began to warn me that it was not an ordinary bison; its surreptitious nature made me believe it was the carrier of 'Yama', the God of death. But He was not to be seen, perhaps because of my torpid eyesight or His invisible sacrament.

"There occurred a sudden flash into my mind that 'Yama' had come to take me away from the worldly life and my fearful waiting lasted only for a few moments. A loud wailing of a girl was heard from some distance away, a very familiar sound it was, and suddenly my fancy of hunting the bison died out completely.

"My horse was heading towards the place from where the cry was heard. But it seemed a long way; the bison was not to be seen anywhere near. The wailing seemed to be driving us away too far. But the horse galloped slowly through the thorny bush and came upon the most dreadful sight.

"What a horrible sight it was! A boa constrictor had almost wrapped a young woman. She was trying to resist it by holding its tail firmly using all her force. The snake was just about to swallow her. Its mouth was opened so wide that it appeared to be a small narrow cave. I couldn't see her face. Her wailing and tremendous struggle to escape made me out of breath, and my heart skipped a beat for a moment.

"Two or three times, I raised my bow to shoot an arrow at the horrifying reptile but feared missing my aim, which would not only be detrimental to the struggling girl but badly hurt my conscience.

"I was in a fix. I wanted to save her and wished earnestly that I could. It seemed I wouldn't get a chance to strike at the snake, but when I got a chance, I didn't hesitate to shoot an arrow at the boa's head. In the wink of an eye, the girl let out a loud scream, and both she and the snake vanished together.

"I tried to read the runes, but the compunction of shooting the arrow at the boa made me confused. What happened to the girl and the boa? Where did they disappear? I couldn't perceive for long. Unusually, my docile horse seemed confused about where to go and became restless. Several times it turned around and seemed to be in bewilderment.

"A cold wind began to blow. The atmosphere seemed to be cloudy. The light gradually became dimmer and dimmer, and soon it began to rain heavily, two or three times the horse neighed. It was the horse's bugle to alert his fellow hunters, but there was no response. They might have been too far and the neigh not heard.

"The rain and the wind brought chilliness along with prostration. I was looking for a way out of the woods. The drizzling and cold wind made the situation all the more severe.

"The horse began to show its uneasiness. But it soon got alerted hearing the girl's cry again. It lent its ears to the girl's wailing and neighed three times. It turned around and lowered its haunch, signalling me to climb aboard and made its way down to the brook, Swaggered down like a newly wedded woman.

"The horse and me quenched our thirst from the brook and took a little rest which made me think that it was thirsty, but the wailing was heard again; we should resume. The cloud had vanished, the wild jasmine smiled beautifully to its lover, and together they danced in the breeze; other plants and shrubs followed. The rustling of the leaves made a chorus.

"The beauty of the landscape, the music of the brook and the gentle breeze made me romantic and took me to my youthful days; filling my heart with nostalgia.

"Seeing the uninvited guests, the beetles murmured, and the squirrels chattered. The fragrance of the jasmine instigated vacillating feelings in my heart. Soon a stench overpowered the fragrance. My horse expanded its nostrils as if something phantasmic and unprecedented had happened. It was reluctant to move forward. The screaming became more distinct and pathetic, and I wished to help, but my horse was stubborn. It turned round and neighed three times when I tried to compel it to move. The wailing became more and more intense and pathetic to melt even the most hard-hearted man's heart. I couldn't turn a deaf ear to it. I saw a vague footpath rarely used by man or animal.

"Carrying my arms, I stepped down. Leaving the horse to graze, I walked along the unwieldy footpath. As I advanced, the stench became more unbearable. I was at the mouth of a den. The stench was from a rotten carcass of an animal lying inside. Near the carcass, there was a big cat on its back, grunting. The wailing was heard from the semi-dark den. The tiger's eye glowed. I saw a girl leaning against the den's wall, frightened so much as if to collapse, shivering. The growling tiger would jump at me at any time if I just moved one step ahead. I wanted to rescue her. But the tiger wouldn't let me in.

"The tiger seemed to be confused about whether the girl or I was to be pounced on first which gave me a few moments to make my spear ready to pierce its trachea, if there was a slight movement, and I waited, holding my breath. As it just began to move towards the girl, I darted the spear at it, and there was a tremendous howling I feared it would split the earth, and nothing could be seen for a moment. To my astonishment, everything had vanished.

"Retrieving the spear that pierced the cave wall, I came down to the brook where I left my horse. But it was not there. I called to it several times, raising my voice, but it didn't turn up. I looked everywhere frantically but could not find it. I was perplexed. I hoped it would come, and waited in panic. My fellow hunters were lost in the woods, and now my horse was also lost, and a fear of calamity began to haunt me.

"I yelled at the top of my voice, and though it echoed several times on the hills, it brought no result. I felt ashamed of my condition. A King without attendants, food or drink, left alone in the woods, perhaps without protection.

"The sun had begun its downward journey leaving the remnants of the day on the western sky. I looked at the mountain top. It was all golden but seemed slightly reddish. The rocky black peak seemed to protrude into the sky with a halo of reddish gold.

"It never dawned upon my timid mind that I was stranded in a dark, dense woods, perilous, and all alone at the late hours of the day. An arduous situation to get out of, it seemed to grab confusion by the scruff of the neck.

"The breezy fragrant evening in the lonely woods taught me that man is lonely in a crisis. There might be several to share the achievements, but none to pick up the gauntlet or share the fiasco.

"Suddenly, I spotted a girl on the rocky peak on the verge. I thought she was going to jump down into the deep valley to end her life. What sudden dejection gripped her mind, or what was the cause of her frustrations? But there was no time to think it over. I thought she would jump if I delayed. It would have been better if I could find my horse. But nowhere could I find it.

"I hastened up from the foothill to the top faster than a horse or the gales. Actually, I was flying though I had no wings at all. I wished I had wings. The girl was there on the summit of the rocky peak of the mountain.

"The panting and sighing wouldn't exhaust me. I had no obstacles on my route. The thorny bushes or creepers wouldn't be a hindrance to me.

"She was in the same position when I reached the peak. I couldn't see her face as she was facing the valley as if to fly down like a Brahmney kite.

"Nearing her quickly, I called her, 'My little daughter… Don't do it. Don't do it.'

"She didn't listen to me, nor look back, or pay heed to my calling. When I got close to her, she skipped down to the deep valley as if never to be seen of again.

"I looked down the valley, but nothing could be seen. My mind became vacant as a nest after the bird had flown away. I sat on the same rock where I lost her, lost in thought, watching the reddish globe slowly sinking.

"In the pitch dark, I couldn't see anything. Leaning towards the rock, resting, I gazed at the starry sky. Of course, there was no moon. Soon the night became active with the centipedes and chafers; the little ones of the frogs also contributed their share. The grunting of the night owls didn't frighten me. Somehow at the last watch of the night, I slipped into the sea of forgetfulness. Neither the absence of kingly pleasures nor the fuss made by the innumerable night cicadas obstructed me from my sleep; perhaps I was too tired owing to the day-long ride with nothing to eat. The pointed and bumpy rock seemed more comfortable than the soft silky mattress of the royal palace. The sheer fatigue and exhaustion might have pushed me into a happy oblivion.

"When I opened my eyes, I was with the tribal people; half-naked, short, dark figures but undoubtedly stout and strong. They gave me food and water. Instead of gold and silver platters, earthen bowls satisfied my thirst and hunger.

"Wild boar's meat was roasted in the fire pit and served hot in the earthen bowls, and the steaming pungent smell of turmeric and chilly penetrating my nostrils made me sneeze. We ate and drank together, and they taught me the feelings of oneness between a hunter and a King.

"'How loving they are!' I said to myself. I couldn't forget their love even now.

"I didn't tell them that I was a King for fear that they would break away from me. They wouldn't have dared to come nearer or take freedom of treating me like one among themselves. Then love and affection would quickly transform into reverence, which would be far away from innocent love.

"But my kingly pride pricked me for having eaten wild meat so voraciously. 'Aren't you the King?' It seemed to be sceptical of my appearance.

"'Why do you think so?' my conscience responded.

"'Your egregious nature. What else?' my pride said.

"It had become so powerful to question even the most discerned, conscience thought. But it was not ready to give in. 'But it's too much,' my conscience said.

"'What? What's too much?' pride raised its voice. It didn't want to wither away.

"'Your haughtiness, what should I say?' my conscience said unemotionally.

"'Oh! How meek you are! Eating wild meat so voraciously! That too with the scum of the earth!' pride mocked at me disgracefully, which pained my conscience much. Its ridicule exceeded all limits.

"'Wasn't it edible to the King?' conscience said innocently.

"'But a King shouldn't behave like that,' pride abruptly stopped halfway.

"'Survival is the most important thing,' my conscience mumbled.

"'Think of the sagacity and reverence you earned through righteousness,' pride began to advise. But my conscience quickly responded, 'Necessity justifies our actions.'

"'You are arguing to cover up your greed,' pride seemed to blame conscience.

"'No, not at all,' my conscience assured.

"'What would the men think if they knew of your fall?' pride querulously asked.

"'What fall?'

"'Your moral deterioration. What else?'

"'I didn't fall,' conscience quickly said.

"'Then, what's this?' Contempt was brimming out from pride.

"'Just for knowing their way of life,' conscience said,

maintaining its calmness though hate was disgorging.

"'But now you stand at the lowest level,' pride said.

"'The foundation lies at the lowest level, you know.' Conscience was not ready for submission. Then it said, 'Living with them is not shameful.'

"'A King should maintain his living standard. That's what I want to remind you,' said pride.

"'I don't agree with your splurging,' said conscience.

"'You are indisposed to kingly zest and pleasures. You shouldn't be twirled about it,' the kingly pride reminded.

"'How can I when the people struggle for a living?' my conscience asked.

"'Oh! A philanthropist has come for service!' Pride laughed at it, but conscience took it as a compliment. It smiled at it simply, not at all sure whether it was a compliment or a mockery that pride intended and never took it as scurrilous.

"The feasting went on without interruption all night. They made me eat sumptuously, and I couldn't turn a deaf ear to it loving their compulsion. Since my wife's mournful departure, I had been devoid of such things which now I couldn't refuse.

"I watched the man serving food to me. I was amazed. His face had a striking resemblance with that of mine. Then I looked at the next one. He, too, had the same face. I passed on my eyes through other faces, one by one, and all of them looked alike. They had faces, forms and shapes taking after mine.

"In the wee hours of the day, the tribesmen began to leave to their homes, and I felt that a portion of me was being lost at each one's departure. I was left alone by the fire pit. No one invited me to join them, nor did I intend to do it. It appeared to me as the funeral pyre, and I would be the guard of the cremation ground, waiting for the arrival of the dead bodies.

"The howling of the cock of 'Yama' foreboding death was heard. I expected the arrival of a dead body soon and waited impatiently.

"The howling of the jackals and the sounds of the flapping of the wings of bats filled the atmosphere with terror.

"I sat beside the lonely pyre thinking upon the trifling and haplessness of human life and the disconsolation I would get nearing my end. The pomp and splendour of my worldly life couldn't give me consolation. Neither the beautiful wives nor the prowess of children could give me consolation. The accumulation of a huge hoard of money, gems and diamonds would seem to be worthless then.

"'Haven't I built a heaven like palace?' my pride rose high. It awoke my slackened mind, which had been alone and dreary.

"'You squandered immeasurable wealth and perseverance of many,' my conscience pointed out.

"'But it holds its head high in this world,' pride boasted arrogantly.

"'The money can be used for the people's welfare or for meeting their basic needs,' conscience said.

"'You always talk about the welfare of the people but forget to live yourself,' pooh-poohed pride.

"'It's the King's duty,' conscience retaliated.

"'What?'

"'Service.'

"Then it was about the mighty military that pride made a ponderous query. 'Don't we possess a powerful military?' pride said.

"'Of course,' conscience said. 'Unless it fights a more powerful army.'

"'You underestimate?' pride complained.

"'No, I am on the right path,' conscience said.

"'Meaning?' Pride was sceptical of conscience's claim.

"'I mean the facts. True facts,' conscience explained.

"'Facts? Are they relevant?' pride asked.

"'Yes. They are relevant as the sun,' my conscience asserted.

"Once the military which was unequalled, and shook even the most dreadful intruders, now lay powerless to the unwittingly coming infiltrators.

"Pride could not say enough when it described the crown and the throne. 'My crown excels all the crowns of the world,' it said.

"Conscience had to agree with it since it was made of solid gold, studded with gems and diamonds, peerless in cost and beauty. 'And the throne which had been not only my pride but the nation's as well. It's fame once had benumbed the far-off world with surprise.'

"The constant journey seeking pleasures allowed and forbidden now, ends in the pyre. The love, lust, and fulfillment of greed for power all turned worthless.

"What was life for me? What it used to be for others? The comparison never came to my perception until the mantle of power fell on my shoulder.

"My life would have been gratified if I could bring about some improvements to my subjects' lives. I used to go in for introspection in those days, I thought.

"The wind blew, bringing chilliness, but of course, no rain. The pyre was so feeble and at the point of extinction. I put some logs of wood that remained nearby on the pyre. As the wind blew, the burning firewood became active again; its flames overpowered the darkness. Soon I began to feel the heat of the pyre.

"The night seemed so long, and I felt that I had been

guarding the pyre pit for so long. 'Life is so ephemeral as the bubble in a water body, for all, not exempting the King or the beggar, whoever it may be,' my conscience said.

"'When his ego melts into thin air, Man knows God better. He identifies that he is just one among the cores of creations He has made. He experiences the oneness among human beings and knows the credentials cohabiting with power are only hollow,' it continued. 'The beggar crawling along the busy street bears the scorching sun or drizzling rain as the King enjoys the gentle breeze by the ornamental fans in the pageantry.'

"'How were the beggars made?' my conscience said to pride, which thought it a mistake.

"'You always think about beggars and vagabonds,' pride said, expressing its contempt.

"'People were thrown into the streets when everything except themselves was lost,' conscience pointed out.

"'How?'

"'They sell what they have at throwaway prices,' conscience said.

"'Why can't they keep their belongings?' pride blamed the poor.

"'Poverty compels them to do so,' conscience said with a sigh. Then it continued, 'Price surge makes them poorer.'

"'It's their fate, I think,' said pride.

"'I don't think so,' said conscience. Then it said, 'Only a few possess the land and its resources.'

"'So, what?' pride arrogantly said.

"'The rightful claimants are abandoned to the unclaimed land,' conscience explained.

"'Who are the rightful claimants?' was pride's query soaked in contempt.

"'The whole living beings of the earth,' conscience had a candid vision.

"Amidst the discussion, there came several men carrying a dead body wrapped in red cloth on a stretcher in the wee hours of the day chanting the names of God. I didn't notice the face of the corpse, for it was all alike to me, whoever it might be.

"They didn't keep the criteria or ritualistic features, but placing the corpse directly on the pyre and putting wood logs into a big heap, the men soon left. They didn't even look at me. What kind of people were they? I thought; I hadn't ever experienced such a humungous ignominy.

"The charring smell of the corpse began to spread all over. The wailing of the bird 'kuthichudu' was heard several times. It all occurred to me that the bird was instructing me to press down the corpse with a staff for effective burning.

"Enjoying the pleasurable warmth of the pyre, I took rest sufficiently away from it and had a nap for some time with a wooden log as my pillow.

"'Oh! You are sleeping on a wood mattress,' ridiculed pride.

"'Everyone lies on wood at his end,' said conscience scrupulously.

"'Mocking me? What sin brought you here?' pride said. It seemed to be bullying my conscience.

"'No, not sin, but His grace,' it responded calmly.

"'Oh! The final phase of your life has come,' remarked pride.

"'Nearing death?' Conscience was sceptical of the remark.

"'You come from the palace amidst pomp and splendour and now lie guarding the pyre.' Pride was seemingly sympathetic.

"'Isn't it a boon? A different experience?' conscience said.

"'Isn't the wooden log softer than the silk mattress?' said pride taking a beating.

"'But it suits well on this occasion,' said conscience.

"'You feel them alike?' said pride.

"'Oh! Yes,' said conscience.

"'Then you are a true recluse,' complimented pride.

"'People are my prime concern,' said conscience.

"'You leave out pleasures like a nincompoop,' pride again ridiculed me.

"'How can I nibble honey when people suffer?' my conscience said.

"'Even a vagabond excels the King,' said pride.

"'In what ways?' asked conscience.

"'In pleasure making,' said pride.

"Burying the hatchet, my conscience said, 'Can't you make it clear?'

"'Oh! Yes. The King never enjoys but is always concerned. He has no time to enjoy,' pride explained.

"'You're right,' conscience agreed. But added, 'He can't derelict his duties.'

"My conscience heard the calls of hunger and the wailing of sufferers. I couldn't keep quiet. So many ventures came to my perception.

"So suddenly and unexpectedly, a strikingly beautiful young woman appeared before me. She was a collection of glories. I was perplexed. It seemed to me that she had emerged directly out of the funeral pyre. I gazed at her in embarrassment for a few moments.

"Her face looked very familiar to mine, but I couldn't identify or remember her name. Somehow it had been forgotten or lost. I tried to pick up the gems of my memory from the sea of oblivion but couldn't remember; her comeliness and vivacity seemed too familiar and endearing.

"Looking keenly, it dawned on me that she resembled my outcast granddaughter, which aroused my curiosity.

"But how could it be possible at the wee hour of the day from such a faraway place?

"Gazing at her for a long time, it occurred to me that she more resembled her mother, which was natural.

"The incineration was nearing its final phase. The body's fat, burning like wicks, was falling to the bed of the burning wood. The smell spread everywhere, enticing the goblins much.

"I wanted to cherish her in my arms or caress her as I felt it was someone dear to me. I wanted to speak to her. But when I went one step closer, she moved two steps away into the dark and slowly disappeared into the woods."

The King disgorged his nightmare but was disgruntled over the safety of his granddaughter.

Everyone who stood nearby was in a frenzy, which the King wouldn't approve of.

"I saw my child in the woods," the King said.

"Your majesty is bed bound. How could you see her in the woods?" The Physician said submissively. But the King wouldn't agree.

"I saw her in the woods with my own eyes," he said.

"Your majesty left her seventeen years ago," said the physician.

"Had I left her?"

"Of course, my Lord."

"With whom?"

"With one Mannanar. It was heard like that," the physician said.

In the meantime, Vasundhara was summoned. Though his querulous words were broken and obstructed several times in his throat, they were signs of fatigue but never tottered with her condescension.

"What have you done with my child?" The King raised his brows at her. She wanted to avoid such difficult situations in front of others.

"My uncle Majesty, Your Lordship, try to remember," she said, skulking. "Seventeen years have passed by. Yet it pricks him," she murmured.

The very thought made her nervous. But she couldn't avoid him, not as easily as before. She should either answer his queries or silence him.

The King's foolish talk and intermittent outbursts might have made the people think he has become preternatural but wouldn't be enough for her malice. Sometimes his talk filled the nights in his harem.

But soon the King became quiescent, as though he knew his ramblings might make people talk.

"These are only hallucinations," whispered the physician to the men gathered around, which gave some solace to Vasundhara.

"I'll prescribe oil to smear on his head for sound sleep," said the physician. But the King insisted on summoning the Mannanar to his presence.

Chapter 16

Captain Nambiar was looking for a chance to meet the King. Vasundhara had made the surveillance too strict even for a house fly to enter. Still, he could meet the King when everybody dozed off in the afternoon. He reverentially submitted the true facts to the King, who had been bedridden so long. He was staring at him. He observed that the King had improved. He could listen and converse in a feeble voice.

Captain Nambiar complacently told him how he had met Rajalakshmi, his granddaughter and her son Aditya Devan.

"The brilliance of Brahma and qualities of Kshatriya are confluent in him," Captain Nambiar said.

The King's face blossomed a little. He took a deep breath. "He'll raise the fame of your kingdom," he assured the King.

The King, a clear clairvoyant, said, "I was misconstrued. The agents of power had erred me badly." His voice was so feeble, but his vision was candid.

"He is proficient in all martial arts, not to say of his skill in firearms," the Captain said, looking at the King's eyes.

"Will the minister and commandant agree?" The old King was suspicious of them. "Of course, If your Lordship confers with them," the Captain answered.

"But Vasundhara?" the King said. The Captain saw the rage and contempt foaming on his face.

"It's your choice," he said as if he had no vested interest.

"Will she obey?" the King asked.

"If the minister and the commandant agree with your leadership, no force on earth can object to your decision," the captain ascertained. "You are a great statesman," he said to raise his pride.

"I'll confer with them," the King whispered. But his words lacked confidence. "It would be better if your Lordship acted soon," the captain said.

It might have irritated the King. "You press me?" The King raised his eyebrows.

"Not at all, my Lordship," The captain said as politely as he could. "It's for the country," he added.

"Will she influence them?" the King asked.

"Who?" said the captain.

"Vasundhara," said the King.

"She may try. But she can't win them over," the captain explained.

"Why?" Still the King was sceptical.

"They have resentment," reasoned the captain.

"Of their own?"

"Exactly, your Lordship."

"Vasundhara is a Svengali with a covetous heart," the King remarked.

"Your Lordship yearned for an able descendant?" the captain was surveying his Lord's mind.

"Of course, but God didn't hear my prayers." The King seemed to be frustrated over the turn of events.

"No, Lord. God heard your prayers," the Captain said.

"How do you know?" the King asked.

"God has sent Aditya Devan to you." The captain was confident of his claim.

"I've been lying for seventeen years."

"But you survived. It's God's grace."

"How long?"

"Until you hand over the lordship to your blood descendant."

"Can I trust your words?"

"You can trust my words so long as the sun and moon exist."

"Are you sure?"

"Oh! Yes. If you receive him with honours."

The King seemed to be tired and needed rest. As the captain was taking leave of him, he said, "I'll think it over and call you soon."

"It's God's providence," said the captain. He bowed to him before he left. He instructed the attendants of the King to be vigilant and tighten the security. He feared that Vasundhara might take extreme steps to retain power.

Though weak, the King kept his word. He conferred with the minister and commandant and decided to revoke the earlier decisions he made in the court. The King withdrew all the powers he had earlier bestowed to Vasundhara and announced his decision to bring Rajalakshmi and her son, Aditya Devan, to the palace with honours.

Flummoxed by the King's decision, Vasundhara was shut up in a room. Her attendants were instructed to take care of her well both day and night. Many were of the opinion that she had got her comeuppance.

Captain Nambiar met the King as per his words. Having seen the pleasant attitude on his face, he felt gratified.

But he had some reservations. "Won't it fuel an inner fight?" the King said as he knew Vasundhara and Rajalakshmi would stir up a hornet's nest.

"It'll subside soon," said the captain.

"How?"

"Under the magic charisma of your grandson, the spat will die down." A ray of hope flashed on the King's royal face.

Orders were issued for the invitation and reception of Rajalakshmi and Aditya Devan to the palace.

Under the pleasant chilly mist blanket, the hillock hadn't awakened. The morning sun hadn't pulled the blanket aside. The people of the hillock were extremely happy since it was an auspicious day for them.

Aditya Devan was to be taken to the palace for the coronation.

He had completed his sixteenth year and possessed every right to be the legal heir apparent of the kingdom.

Kodanddi's family had moved back to the hillock soon after the tribal kingdom was crushed and the tribals retreated to the deep forests.

Peasants were happy to welcome them. Sixteen years had changed them a lot. His fellow man had maintained Kodanddi's home and premises, and everything was the same as it had been left sixteen years ago.

Vellachi had become too old to walk. Her hair had become grey, and her face wrinkled. Yet they could identify her. Kodanddi was in his middle age. Rajalakshmi had become lean, and her complexion had diminished a little.

Aditya Devan had become the centre of attention, as though he had stepped out of another planet.

Children gathered around to touch him and talk to him, which he didn't object to. He smiled at them, touched them lovingly and spoke to them endearingly.

The huts on the hillock were cleaned and smeared with cow dung. The downhill path was made clean and festooned with flowers and leaves. The whole community had turned up to bid the prince a fitting farewell.

The bugle signalling the start was heard from the foothill.

Kasthuri and Aditya Devan went to seek the blessings of Vellachi and Kodanddi. Together they touched Vellachi's feet.

"Grandma, you come with us," Aditya Devan beseeched to his grandmother.

Vellachi embraced her grandson and kissed him on his forehead, caressed through his thick curly black hair and spoke to him lovingly.

"Amma, let's go. No need for any more sufferings. Come with us," Rajalakshmi pleaded.

Vellachi couldn't say anything but hugged her, falling into tears with a sobbing heart. Kasthuri also sobbed.

Tears rolled down her cheeks, and they were consoling each other. Vellachi was so upset she looked to the ground.

"Mom, you gave me life. It was my second birth. As a true mother, you fed me and nurtured me. Mom, you come with us," Kasthuri again beseeched earnestly.

Tears made her clothes wet. They were wiping their tears from each other. "I'll implore Kodanddi. Both of you come. I can't get along without you."

Kasthuri walked to Kodanddi, who was sitting on the raised platform of his hut with a heavy heart and head.

"Kodanddi," she called him in a heart-melting voice. She couldn't face him.

He, too, couldn't see her tears. Both were looking to the ground. Kasthuri said, "You come with us with our mother," she pleaded.

When Aditya Devan touched his feet, Kodanddi said, "Make sure, you keep the trust of the people." Then he hugged him and kissed him on his head.

"How can I live without you?" Kasthuri said.

Kodanddi slowly raised his eyes and looked at her. Their eyes met. They wanted to say many things. Their love, their ramblings in the woods, and so many things not easily forgotten, perhaps that may last even in their succession of births.

But she had to go. They heard the bugle again. Her son would have to perform his 'Raja-Dharma'. Then she would have to take her turn too.

"What is life to me without you?" Kasthuri said. Her tears trickled down her cheeks as she looked lovingly at him.

Kodanddi didn't say anything. He looked at Vellachi, who was sobbing.

"A true prince never weeps; you had said to me once. He smiles even at the moment of his death," Kodanddi said to them.

Kasthuri thought that they would go with them. She took their silence as affirmative. Of course, they had no energy to deny her.

The peasants with women and children plodded down along the footpath. Rajalakshmi and Aditya Devan in the middle. They thought that Kodanddi and Vellachi would be in the rear. The steep downy path forbade them from looking back, which they could do on reaching the foothill, but they couldn't find them anywhere in their vicinity.

"Did you see my Kodanddi?" Kasthuri said to many. The people looked at each other. They felt pity seeing Kasthuri searching for Kodanddi, her eyes turbid and cheeks swelled up.

"Kodanddi," Kasthuri cried out at the top of her voice. But it couldn't reach the top of the hill. The hills echoed, "Kodanddi... Kodanddi..." but no response was heard. Perhaps Kodanddi might have responded from the top of the hillock.

Not seeing them, Kasthuri and Aditya Devan tried to return to the hillock. But the army of men prevented them, saying that the auspicious time was going to cease, and it was high time for them to start. They promised to bring them later.

They couldn't think of a life without Kodanddi and Vellachi. But the remembrance of Raja-Dharma prevented them from going back. Kasthuri felt as if her heart had been plucked out of her.

At the foot of the hill, women welcomed them with decorated platters having lamps and flowers.

A decorated chariot drawn by seven horses was arranged for the delegate prince and his mother. Twenty-one horse riders with swords and shields would accompany them.

Rajalakshmi and Aditya Devan looked everywhere for Kodanddi and Vellachi. But they couldn't be seen anywhere among the peasants. They looked back at the hillock and saw them waving their hands under the Alstonia scholaris tree a long distance away.

As the rising sun ascended the eastern horizon, Aditya Devan's chariot, accompanied by the horse riders, moved forward. The hills resounded to the sound of the horses' hooves.